AVANT–POP
FICTION FOR A DAYDREAM NATION

AVANT-POP

FICTION FOR A DAYDREAM NATION

EDITED BY LARRY McCAFFERY

BLACK ICE
BOOKS

BOULDER • NORMAL

First edition
First printing 1993

Published by Fiction Collective Two with support given by the English Department Publications Unit of Illinois State University, the English Department Publications Center of the University of Colorado at Boulder, and the Illinois Arts Council

Address all inquiries to: Fiction Collective Two, c/o English Department Publications Center, Box 494, University of Colorado at Boulder, Boulder, CO 80309-0494

Avant–Pop: Fiction for a Daydream Nation
Larry McCaffery, Editor

ISBN: 0–932511–72-4, Paper, $7.00

Produced and printed in the United States of America

Cover image: John Bergin
Book design: Jean C. Lee

For Kathy Acker ("that's with a 'k,' Mac!") and Mark Leyner (the hottest and densest dude around—glad to have been around when you started expanding)

Judge said, "What have you got in your defense son?"
Fifty-seven channels and nothin' on."

—Bruce Springsteen,
"57 Channels (and Nothin's On)"

To tell the truth and to shoot well with arrows: *that is Persian virtue.*

—Friedrich Nietzsche, *Ecce Home*

CONTENTS

ILLUSTRATIONS

ACKNOWLEDGEMENTS

Grateful acknowledgement is made to the following publications in which some of the stories in this book originally appeared:

Kathy Acker, "Politics," in *Politics,* © 1973 Kathy Acker;

John Bergin, "The Water Tower," in *ashes,* ©1990 John Bergin;

Samuel R. Delany, "On the Unspeakable," *Everyday Life,* No. 2, August 1988. Eds., Chris Tysh and George Tysh;

Eurudice, "Once Upon a Woman," *f/32,* © 1991 Eurudice Kamviselli;

Mark Leyner, "I'm Writing About Sally," in *I Smell Esther Williams,* ©1982 Fiction Collective;

David Matlin, from *How the Night Is Divided,* © 1993 David Matlin. Printed by permission of MacPherson Publishers;

Richard Meltzer, "Okay With You," "Days of Wine and Beer," and "Premonitions of the Night," © Richard Meltzer;

Derek Pell, "The Elements of Style," excerpted from "The Elements of Style," *Fiction International* 22, 1992; © 1987, 1988, 1992 Derek Pell;

Harry Polkinhorn, "Consumimur Igni," (in Spanish translation) in *En La Línee De Fuego,* 1990 T.erra Adendro, Mexico City;

Stephen Wright, from "Getting Happy," from *Going Native* by Stephen Wright. © Stephen Wright. Printed by permission of Farrar, Straus & Giroux, Inc.

Special thanks to Kathy Acker for lending me her image (or one of them), collaborating with me on "Tsunami," and providing the names and addresses of several contacts that turned into contributors to *Avant-Pop*. Thanks to other unacknowledged "Tsunami" collaborators, including Dashiell Hammett, Terry Allen, Humphrey Bogart, and Gene Kelly. Thanks, too, to all of *Avant-Pop*'s contributors for their enthusiasm, trust, and generosity (many of them took major pay-cuts to allow their work to appear here). I appropriated "avant-pop" from a wonderful Lester Bowie jazz album. Ronald Sukenick helped drag the "avant-pop" term out of the junkyard of my memory in a phone conversation. Sukenick and Curt White both provided encouragement and made invaluable editorial suggestions at every stage of *Avant-Pop*'s evolution. Jean C. Lee provided the technical know-how to get the shaggy beast of this ms. into appropriate formal wear. Jim Edwards, Cyberspace Technician and Overseer of San Diego State University's Faculty Room, provided mega-doses of technical assistance, patience, and much-needed words of calm when the walls seemed to be crumbling down. Jim McMenamin supplied more direct creative input, along with a place to crash, thrash, and trash ideas for the anthology. Takayuki Tatsumi and other Tokyo-based friends and editors helped sharpen my concept of *Avant-Pop* during my 1992 summer NEH-supported stay in Japan. David Blair's remarkable film, *Wax, or the Discovery of Television Among the Bees*, provided near-nightly inspirations of a nature too mysterious to specify. As always, it was Sinda Gregory who gave me the most important daily boosts (when I needed them) and busts (in the chops, when they were called for); without her daily supply of sanity and passion, *Avant-Pop* would have pooped out on the launching pad.

"TSUNAMI..."

INTRODUCTION BY LARRY McCAFFERY

I first heard Postmodern called Postmortem by a tattooed postfeminist mucker named Kathy Acker in my office just after the first tremors in the Pacific started making my literary seismograph go haywire. She also called deconstruction de*cunt*struction. I didn't think anything of what she had done to the literary categories at the time, but later I heard commercial fiction editors and tenured critical theorists who could manage their s's and c's give it the same pronunciation. I still didn't see anything in it but the meaningless sort of humor that used to make richardsnary the thieves' word for dictionary.

Of course, I wasn't seeing most things clearly in those days. I was daydreamin', hell, we all were—sleepwalking through roles that felt comfortable enough but didn't provide much in the way of...*action*. I like to think now that just before going on the nod back in the early 80s, Americans had somehow at least gotten it together enough to ask for a wake-up call—that way at least the wave of avant-pop literary disruption dumped on our heads was something we welcomed, had in fact invited to happen. But frankly, my dears, the avant-pop gang don't give a damn whether they've been sent a fancy invite card or not. Don't let their kookie surface textures or wacko sense of sicko humor mislead you into lumping them in with all "counter-culture wimps" you see hanging out on the street corners trying to look tough—you know, the ivory tower academics, the limo Marxists, bland workshop bore-ons, and commodified "radicals" you see these days. I mean, A-P guys are hardened professionals—a new breed of pop-cultural demolition artists, cultural terrorists who've put in their hours of training in front of the boob tube with all regular zombies so they can know the enemy's terrain, the pop figures who live there, the local lingoes. They're like the Green Beret—the Special Forces unit developed by the U.S. Army to serve in 'Nam as counter-insurgency specialists. And as in 'Nam, A-P exists because the kind of weapons, tactics, and know-how used by ordinary writers ain't gonna cut it with what we're up against today.

But I'm getting ahead of myself. Let me set the scene of that first night by sketching in a few details and then you connect the dots....

I'd been sitting in my office, keeping company with a fifth of cheap whiskey and a review copy of the latest anthology of "bold and daring" new fiction—the kind of slick-looking trade paperbacks that began showing up in bookstores back in the early 90s after it became obvious there was now this whole audience of jaded yuppies, tenured-radicals, and graduate-students-with-attitudes—people still looking for an angry fix but now willing to settle for a Madonna video or a Guns 'N Roses tee-shirt (both retailing for 26 bucks). I'd only agreed to review this collection of ludicrous garbage after my department chair surprised me one afternoon by reaching into her desk and pulling out a .44 mag in a solid steel caste—thereby putting a whole new twist to the phrase "Publish or perish."

So, you know the scene: me in my swivel chair with the bound galleys and sweat stains coming through my wilted shirt, the overflowing ashtray, the desk cluttered with student papers and quality literary magazines and small press publications, the muggy heat being slowly redistributed by the overhead fan, the sound of the rain coming down the drainpipe mixing with the shadows and the whiskey and a kind of melancholy ache I get whenever I come across the sort of pre-packaged "dangerous writing" these days. I was only a few pages into the anthology and already fighting off the droopy eyelids and yawns when my department secretary who'd been working late that night preparing my tenure-review files stopped by my office. "Yes, sweetheart?"

"There's a girl wants to see you." She has a rich throaty voice that made me think of Bacall back in her 40s heyday. "Her name's Kathy."

"A student or a customer?"

"Hard to tell. You'll want to see her anyway: she's a knockout."

"Shoo her in, darling," I said. "Shoo her in."

A voice said, "Thank you," so softly that only the purest articulation made the words intelligible, and then a woman came through the doorway. It was quite an eyeful: she advanced slowly, looking directly at me with brown eyes that were both shy and probing, her steps hindered by black dominatrix-style stiletto-heels retrofitted into motorcycle boots. Black rainwater spilled down over her black leather jacket and black leather pants, leaving behind what looked like pools of blood and ink on the red linoleum floor. She was average height and pliantly slender, without angularity anywhere except where dog-eared copies of paperback books and literary journals jutted out from the numerous zippered pockets in her jacket and pants. Her body had the sculpted curves and surprising textures I associated in those days with female wrestlers—an impression that somehow didn't match up with the copy of Foucault's *Discipline and Punish* she was clutching in her right hand. The punked-out hair curling out from under her black sweat-band was a rainbow variety of red, her full red lips reddest of all.

I rose and indicated the oaken armchair beside my desk. She sat down on the edge of her seat and began, "Dr. McCaffery," and I got my first glimpse of that piercing smile, the gob of bronze embedded in one of her white front teeth somehow transforming her face from *Vanity Fair* good looks into something out of a Mapplethorpe exhibit.

"Why don't you call me Mac?" I said, trying to put her more at ease. "Now what can I do for you?"

She caught her breath and looked at me. Then she swallowed and said hurriedly, "A friend of mine who works at Small Press Distributions over in Berkeley gave me your name and address. I didn't know where else to turn. Could you—?—I thought—I—that is—have you read Calvino's *The Castle of Crossed Destinies?*" With very delicate movements, she began to arrange her books and magazines on my cluttered desk. There were a lot of pockets and zippers to go through.

I smiled and nodded as if I understood, but pleasantly, as if nothing serious was involved. The Calvino reference, puzzling at first, seemed like an invite for me to devise a narrative from the stuff she had laid in front of me like tarot cards. Seeing as how she didn't seem too eager to supply me with any of her own close textual readings, I started rummaging through the stuff for clues—checking the inscriptions and marginal comments, seeing what pages had been folded or seemed unusually worn, the usual sort of lit crit detective work.

You didn't need to be a Private E to see that it was an unusual assortment: critical studies by the trendiest poststructural suspects (Barthes, Bataille, Jameson, Lacan, Baudrillard, etc.); Bill Vollmann's *Fathers and Crows* (the latest installment on his septology of "Dream Novels"); Harold Jaffe's *Madonna and Other Spectacles*,;Stephen Wright's Beckett-meets-the-Munsters take on the UFO phenomenon, *M-31*; something old by Samuel R. Delany (*Babel 17)* and something new (one of his post-Derridean sword-and-sorcery-and-semiotics series about *Neveryon*); rare editions of Derek Pell's late 70s collage masterpieces, the *Dr. Bey'*series, were stacked on top of *3-D Sade*—a plastic case containing a bloodied copy of Sade's *Justine* through which Pell's alter ego, Norman Conquest, had a huge nail; wild comic book stuff by several of the leading underground graphic novelists (mostly sicko surrealist stuff like Feret's *Phoenix Restaurant* and John Bergin's *Bone Saw*); next to a couple of Harry Polkinhorn's journals devoted to "border writing" (*Atticus Review, Fiction International)*; she'd also lined up Native American po mo books (a couple of Gerald Vizenor's Native American "trickster" novels, Misha's *Red Spider, White Web*); and Eurudice's *f/32*, the scandalous (but American-Book Award) bildungsroman (with Lacanian overtones) literally narrated by a cunt.

Next came two anthologies I'd edited, opened to specific selections: Rob Hardin poems from *Storming the Reality Studio* and Mark Leyner's "i was an infinitely hot and dense dot," the lead story in the *Mississippi Review* cyberpunk issue in '88 which helped Leyner, the most intense and in a certain sense the most significant young prose writer in America (but also now buffed, and carrying high literary explosives), gain entry into an unsuspecting commercial publishing scene without having to pass through any metal detectors. Rounding things out were manuscripts by several promising new kids on the literary block—a crazed Faulkner-meets-Burroughs manuscript that Doug Rice had submitted as a Ph.D. thesis somewhere back in the Midwest; a story about transsexuality by a San Francisco lady-boy whose moniker was Jill St. Jacques; and a huge pile of pages about some crazy Indian living out in the California desert with hummingbirds, monkeys and rose bushes for companions by this guy named David Matlin, whose return address was listed as some prison in up state New York.

In short: not the sort of thing you'd expect a lady-wrestling, motorcycle mama to be carrying around with her for bed-time reading.

I'd been glancing through the evidence with the kind of furious, silent concentration that produces a satisfying turd. And sure enough, pretty soon a narrative began to emerge: something about an extended family that rivaled the Mia Farrow brood in terms of racial, economic, and age-diversity—only the kids were all innovative writers; the parents were 60s postmodernists—troublemaking radicals who'd dropped outta sight in the mid-70s once the Gulf and Western accountants who pulled the chains of all the commercial publishers discovered what kind of medicine they'd been mixing up down in their basement.

Growing up must have been pretty odd—George Sand, Monique Wittig and Burroughs for bedtime reading, Patti Smith and Stein as pin-up girls for the walls, thinking Rambo was some punked-out French poet. Anyway, by the the late 80s, they'd signed a pact in blood to carry out a kamikaze Mission Impossible/Dirty Dozen assignment: relying on their parents' yellowed maps (passed on for over a hundred years by generations of the avant-garde clan) and state-of-the-art weapons originally hand-made for 'em by Billy Burroughs back in the first postmodernist counter-insurgency uprisings of the 60s (brutally suppressed during the 70s), the A-P family's attack-plan relied on the use of concentrated bits of aesthetic disruption to blast through the cocoon of habituation imprisoning most Americans (a cocoon mostly composed of dangerously addictive pop cultural stereotypes, cliched attitudes, reductive role models, and narrative formulas that the media was passing out to people just like the Brits did with opium to the Chinese). Once gaining entrance, the A-P gang hoped to rescue the badly malnourished creative imaginations, and lead 'em the fuck out of the banal prisons they'd grown so comfortable curled up inside of.

All this was obvious enough. Only one thing seemed to be missing: where was Kathy Acker, the tough, street-wise dame who was the obvious choice to play the role of heroine in this tale of guerrilla resistance against the logic of the late capitalist media industry? Across the desk, my client decided to give me something new to chew on by taking off her leather jacket and giving me a muscular demonstration of how her tattoos could be seen as a self-empowering sign system that she was perfectly in control of. Had my secretary mentioned if this lady in distress spelled her name with a "C" or a "K" anyway?

"Suppose you tell me about it, from the beginning, and then we'll know what needs doing. Better begin as far back as you can."

"That was New York."

"Yes..."

Once she got started, her story spilled out of her in the kind of non-linear stream of disconnected phrases, references to people and events, bits of dialogue and literary allusions that you used to find in Barthelme or Burroughs back in the 60s. Or Acker in the 90s:

"...serious literary journals didn't pay anything and no creative writing program was going to hire somebody like mommy or daddy...scolded for appropriating Shakespeare in my second grade fiction writing contest but I could tell he was proud...'you can't just do the blank page when you're 12—it took Beckett 70 years to get to the blank page!!!!'...pretty weird having this goddess from Crete as a step-sister, but it turned out she was also interested in reclaiming the word 'cunt'...should've realized it was a set up—no way a commercial house is going to put up that kind of dough for an anthology of our work...got to the reception late, but as soon as I got there, I could tell something was...locked from the inside but nobody...no word for a week...the run-around from the academic specialists assigned to the case...way he said 'cyberpunk' like it was unclean made me want to shove that pipe up his ass...'look, lady, you'd be better off hanging out at the gym with your friends than worrying your pretty little head with'...guy's voice leaking down the hall in the morgue saying, 'You didn't hear? lady, I hate to tell ya this, but the avant-garde is *dead*!'...'what's a nice writer like you doing in a science fiction bookstore, anyways!?'...laughed at me in the inter-library-loan...'Graphic novels?' he said, wiping his greasy chin and leering, 'don't you mean *comic books?'*...you're the last chance I have."

This had gone on for a while like one of those late Celine novels when I finally cut her off. She was one fast and loose gal, alright—the scary sexy kind that makes some guys want to go fishing. Me, I just poured myself another tumbler of bourbon and started rolling a fag with the same deliberate care I used in the library when tracking down some renegade footnote, sifting a measured quantity of tan flakes down into curved paper, spreading the flakes so that they lay equal at the ends with a slight depression in the middle, thumbs rolling the paper's inner edge down and up under the outer edges as forefingers pressed it over, thumbs and fingers sliding to the paper cylinder's ends to hold it even while my tongue licked the flap, left forefinger and thumb pinching their end while right forefinger and thumb smoothed the damp seam, right forefinger and thumb twisting their end and lifting the other to my mouth, all the while thinking how I'd have to be crazy or bored or desperate to work on this case. But by the time I had picked up the pigskin and nickel lighter that had fallen to the floor and drawn a deep hot drag from my fag, my mouth had decided to say, "Okay, I'll take the case. But, look, let's lay some ground rules here."

"I don't know who it was up in Berkeley who mighta been whispering the kind of sweet nothings in your ear that would bring you to the lunatic fringe part of the neighborhood, but now that you're here, there's a few things you should know straight off. One: with the kind of bread the state pays me for being an English professor, the moonlighting I do as a Private E has got to bring in enough dough to keep me stocked in books and literary magazines—with maybe a little left over for airfare to a few conventions. The bottom line is: I don't come cheap. I get 10 bucks a day, plus expenses, *and* unlimited Xerox and mailing privileges, a Tuesday/Thursday schedule, and *no committee work!!* Two: no dice to any deal that takes me outside my own literary neighborhood. Now maybe this neighborhood is inhabited mostly by literary odd balls, kooks—guys and gals who used to live in the underground until they got evicted back during the 80s, when all the federal grants and support for the arts started drying up. Most of 'em are criminals who don't think twice about what literary convention they have to off if they can see an aesthetic advantage to it. It's a fucking jungle out there alright; you step outside your turf, chances are good you'll get mugged by some tight-ass reviewer out to look cute.

"What I'm saying is: you sure you want my kind of Private E instead of one of those commercial editors who wears suits and takes you out for sushi? I specialize in the true weirdos, throwbacks I call 'em, writers who are out there on the wire because they like the danger and they feel that playing safe ain't good for them or their audience.

"I mean don't get me wrong—I've been living out here in the darkness on the postmodern edge of town so long, the loneliness and weirdness feels like home by now. Hell, offer me a place with a linear plot, a strong overall sense of character development, and an epiphanic conclusion that draws everything together and produces a pleasing sense of closure, and my instincts are to light out for the territories. I've done enough time working for literary mags to know what part of the river to check for underground writers who've turned their backs on their pals and decided to go mainstream—wearing a pair of concrete galoshes; I can tell you which jazz joints the old-timers like Coover, Pynchon, Federman and Sukenick are likely to be hanging out in, and which rave the younger guys like Cruz, Leyner, Eurudice and

Vollmann like to get ecstatic at.

"Let me put it for you country simple: I'm no good hustling the big money books or the specialty come-on's in flashy covers. But if you got a problem that requires an off-beat, twisted sensibility, somebody who knows where the real postmodern action is going down, well, maybe you came to the right place."

I was going pretty good, and I could see from the expression in her eyes that my overture had jump-started her rhythm section and she was ready to pull me out onto a dark dance floor. I stabbed out my fag.

"Let's see if I catch your drift. You've risked coming over here because you have some missing relatives and you're desperate enough to try anything—even some guy who's last review started out "Larry McCaffery is either an idiot or a lunatic, and someone should stop him"—right? You keep running into dead ends with the big-name editors, creative writing profs, and contemporary fiction specialists. Nobody's heard of any writers matching your descriptions, right? It's like they fell off the earth, right? So now you're here because every respectable editor is sick of your pestering and then somebody told you that if all else fails there is this guy down in the boondocks who specializes in missing writers cases.

A light in Kathy's eyes pulled me in and I headed straight for the roadblocks and the signs marked "DO NOT ENTER" and "DANGER." She rose and for several long moments we stood there silently. I honestly didn't know at that moment if I wanted to take her into my arms and comfort her or catch her off guard with one of those straight right hand leads that Ali surprised Norton with in the second fight. It must have been while I was contemplating my options that she made her move.

I don't recall much about the next few seconds. The next thing I knew, everything was topsy turvy: Kathy now sitting behind my desk, browsing through my address book and secret editorial computer files. Me sitting in her chair, a little embarrassed, a little afraid, the wrists clasped behind my back already aching from the cuffs she'd somehow slipped on while I was making my exit lines. Once we started the next round of our dialogue, though, things *really* started getting screwy.

"Look, Mac," Acker was saying, all trace of weakness, confusion and everything else gone from her voice so her voice kept disappearing, "don't you think that this sexism thing has gone far enough? Under the sign of racism, everyone who has any color skin is a victim—I am talking about you and me." She started to masturbate because, basically, she liked being alone. "Likewise, under the sign of sexism, men, women and everyone else are fucked.

"Do away with the whole thing.

"I mean," she whimpered, backtracking, retracking, trying to remember what she had just said, if she meant anything, and barely remembering anything because her pussy was starting to smell, "well, I mean something. I mean that I've got a pussy and pussies are forever. But a pussy is a pussy is a pussy. It's not dominatrix or submissive, a tyrant or a victim. Get off it, buddy: I am not interested in whipping anyone. I can't even tell myself what to do and why should I want to, when I smell so good?" Then she became lost trying to hide her nostrils in her pussy.

But this cunt couldn't manage to succeed at anything. Even masturbation. "Listen," she murmured, having failed, "if there are any rules, even literary ones, they aren't mine. Or yours. So they must be the rules of chaos, chance, the body. Throw the rest out, it's made up anyway. Have you heard the new Sinead O'Conner?

"And as far as rules go, all there is is missing evidence: Pirates, smells, and foreignness. Everyone is always missing."

The idiot in female clothes named Acker was now making mewling noises. "So when are you going to play with me and make me giggle? I love being happy."

As you can imagine, my reaction to this was pretty mixed. Two counterpunctal voices struggled for control of my inner libretto. The hoarse rain-and-butt stained growl (c. Tom Waits of *Heartattack* and *Vine*) I used as a lit crit and detective was saying things like, "Ignore this dame! She's as flaky as a soil sample from the Mojave. Or maybe she slipped some Maui Wowie into that last fag you was smoking. She's trying to undermine the source of your authority as classical dick/lit crit; where most people see chaos and mystery, you read the clues of reality/fiction and demonstrate that order always can be restored via the process of rational analysis and empirical observation." Meanwhile, the postmodernist side of me was spewing forth a delirious babel that sounded like Diamanda Galas's "Wild Women with Steak Knives": This broad with her nose up her pussy is reinforcing Nietzsche's dictum (at the conclusion of *Ecce Home*): 'My genius is in my nostrils.' The entropy and chaos coursing through your dick and her clit is the underlying principle of the universe, not rationality. Reason is an outdated, phallocentric system of anal-compulsive delusion devised by men so they don't have to contemplate how much they'll stink after they're dead. Besides, as Brian McHale notes in his influential study *Postmodern Fiction*, detective fiction is a modernist mode inappropriate in the age of chaos theory, Heisenberg, relativity, quantum mechanics, and Kurt Godel. "Give it up, Mac!"

In the end, well, it was no contest. I cranked up the amps on the postmodern signal as high as Pete Townsend used to do before he started going deaf, thereby drowning out all traces of rationality, coherent narrative trajectory, and stable identity. Soon my cuffs were off and Kathy and I found ourselves gloriously freed from all those staid rules about who sat where, who had a dick and who had a cunt, who had the power and who had to kneel down, who thrusts, who heaves. Things started feeling a lot more comfortable right away. The first thing I did was shit-can my half-full tumbler of cheap hootch and pull out a bottle of Chivas Regal that had been waiting for just a such a moment; then I reached up, turned off the overhead fan, and found myself finally able to say what I'd wanted to for so long: "It's too goddamn *hot* in here! I'm tired of these embarrassing sweat stains!! Let's turn on the air-conditioner!"

Kathy was in perfect sync with what was in the air as she reached down and announced, "And I finally get to slip off these uncomfortable motorcycle boots and put on my sneakers!"

It didn't take me long to get the hang of activities my two-dimensional role as a romantic-tough-guy-loner had never given me the opportunity to try. While my left hand reached into my lap and began masturbating with slow, steady and wondrously pleasurable strokes, my right hand reached for my lap-top and began typing up the opening to this introduction; meanwhile I was dictating an avant-poop pono porn memo to my department secretary, who looked surprised only for the few moments it took for her to appraise the situation and get into the spirit of things by donning Kathy's black leather jacket, and vigorously plunging the strap-on she'd triumphantly released from its captivity behind my dusty copy of *The Fairie Queen* into whatever orifices seemed most readily available (and there were plenty of options). Neither she nor Kathy seemed particularly embarrassed by the profusion of poppycock—pop-porn and purple-pickled pecker juice—pouring from my mouth and dick, respectively.

Did I feel a sense of remorse that the detective-novel premise I had labored so mightily to ease off its launching pad was now veering crazily off its original course? Hell, no! The truth is that the white light and white heat of those early Mercury rockets blowing apart a few seconds after blast-off had always seemed more interesting to me (and a lot more satisfying from a personal standpoint) than watching the later "successful" Apollo launchings. As far as I was concerned, those out-dated aspects of old-fashioned realism could just go *fuck themselves*!

But what about my obligation to help Kathy locate her loony literary relatives? After all, in a universe governed (if governed at all) only by Gnostic demi-urges and the second law of thermodynamics, didn't a man have to keep his word once he'd agree to enter into a game whose rules, even if they were arbitrary, were the only thing preventing a complete abandonment to the dark diceman? But *nix on that!! All bets were off if you discovered the game had been rigged in ways nobody'd tipped you off to when you put everything out there on lucky number 7 !!*

Luckily, though, the sense that this existential dilemma had pushed me precariously close to the edge of an abyss which offered no option but to hurl oneself off in a defiant leap of faith was greatly diminished by the comforting sound of my Apple NTX2 Lazer Printer rhythmically printing out hard copy of all the relevant information contained in my

File-Maker Pro "Avant-Pop" files. This meant that Kathy would soon not only have each family member's home and business address, along with their fax and phone numbers, and birthdays, but also, via a simple cross-reference system available on the new 5.2 software, their e-mail codes, MLA Directory Listings, condom sizes, and an alphabetically arranged listing of all the porn movies they'd rented during the previous 18 months at Blockbuster Video

"Isn't that finally avant-poop's principal point?"I said to Kathy somewhat later as she and my department secretary were about to head out into the rain onto highway 61 aboard Kathy's Yamaha 750. "You introduce the conventions so you can FUCK with them, show everybody there're other options, find openings in the system that will let the wind blow back your hair, cause the night's bustin' open and these two lanes can take you anywhere?" I could barely make myself heard over the engine noise.

"One last thing," I shouted as they edged out onto Thunder Road, "what password should we use to refer to your family's covert literary operation? 'New Wave'?"

"Already anachronistic—and a cliche to boot." They were almost out of ear shot and the rain was making it difficult to see clearly.

"And people would associate you guys with the 60s," chimed in my department secretary.

"How about 'Next Wave' then?"

"Even worse," said Kathy. "It's already been used as the come-on for those awful Vintage or Viking contemporary series."

I began to jog after them, pleased with my foresight in buying a pair of John Lennon-inspired Nike tennis shoes, but depressed at the way our story was ending. "I guess we have to can the whole 'wave' metaphor. Too bad. I liked that motif of a force jolted suddenly into existence by powerful subterranean forces indetectable to radar or satelite surveillance, then gathering strength from collective action, waiting until just the right moment before it zooms in from the horizon and BOOM!! Soon nothing around but clean beaches and Deborah Kerr making out with Burt Lancaster as the foam swirls around them." I was losing ground when Kathy turned towards me for the last time and spoke.

"Tsunami!" The word was almost lost in the roar. Then the blackness of the two night riders merged with the other blackness.

I stood there for a moment repeating Kathy's mysterious term, mantralike, to see how it sounded: "Tsunami... tsunami...tsunami." Yes, the force was with me. I ambled back to my office, whistling "Singing in the Rain."

BLESSED

STEPHEN WRIGHT

What an evening. Perry's sensibility felt embarked on a perilous voyage, internal gyro beginning a wobble premonitory of on-your-back illness or another, less comprehensible mode of mental deficit where your remaining wits (a slapstick posse of armed clowns) find it necessary to circle the wagons and start rationing the ammo. His mood was not lightened by his initial glimpse of tonight's star who had groomed and costumed himself into a passable likeness of the standard caucasian Christ with the shoulder length chestnut tresses, the manicured beard, the brown eyes, the white robe, the leather sandals, the complete complement of Hollywood props. It was a role Mr. Dyne had been in training for since puberty, crawling between the bedraggled tomato plants in his indulgent parents' backyard garden, homemade cross lashed to his scalp, a series of Polaroids memorializing the event now circulating among the rowdy and the randy gathered to witness the transfiguration of those crude rehearsals into an elaborate full-dress and somewhat revised version of the four Gospels.

On the patio, to Perry's surprise, stood a blazing grill the size of a billboard table, its bloody array of spitting meats attended by a sweaty ox-like man who had quit a promising career in pro wrestling to run security for Cool Cat Productions—Freya's fame, though quartered off the blaring midway, still of sufficient intensity to attract its share of dangerous bugs. This illustrious worthy, barbecue implements in tattooed hands, posed behind the crackling flames, smoke streaming over him in a constant rising curtain, the image of Vulcan at his forge.

Ingewald, the dwarf, sat forlornly on the grass, vomiting noisily into a silver ice bucket. A fellow countryman of the Baldurssons, he roomed in a spartan basement cell (no pictures, no plants, no windows) beneath the Rainbow Bridge. He spent his days reading empirical philosophy, his nights on the phone with relatives back in Reykjavik. He had appeared in more than two dozen videos and was beloved by sexers of every taste.

"I don't feel so good, Perry, I'm afraid I might do something bad."

"What are you talking about, you're incapable of giving a bad performance?"

"I don't mean videos, asshole, I mean in real life."

"How bad?"

"Things, you know. My head's tight. I've lost breathing space. I wake up in tears."

"I felt like that once."

"Really? What'd you do?"

"Isn't it obvious? I killed myself."

Perry had to move smartly to avoid being splattered by a flung bucket of multicolored stomach chunks, simuitaneously dodging other wet matter that happened to be flying through his air space from sources unknown. The earlier prevailing tone of controlled riot seemed to be balancing now on the edge of something worse. There were men wearing tube socks as penis sheaths and women with G-strings fashioned out of dental dams. There were fistfights in the hydrangea, orgasms among the croquet wickets. Freya was over by the picnic table, setting up The Last Supper scene, the participants in sundry intemperate states of mind too busy clowning around with the hot dogs and the pickles to pay much attention until Mr. Dyne, in a character-breaking outburst, began berating his apostles, the flux of unexpected obscenities positively exhilarating, for gum-chewing, talking out of turn, and touching one another inappropriately. Freya handed Perry the camcorder and told him to shoot on his own initiative, the theme of this scene: food as sex and sacrament. Perry's main impression: John the Baptist had an extremely long tongue.

The rest of the evening proceeded at a hallucinatory pace.

The rose bushes along the western wall of the house served as the garden of Gethsemane where an ex-Bronco fullback betrayed Mr. Dyne with a highly enthusiastic kiss involving an exchange of bodily fluids Freya frowned upon but endorsed by the hearty applause of deranged onlookers.

Pontius Pilate, a six-foot Valkyrie in drag (another rumored dalliance of Freya's shipped in from the homeland) ordered Mr. Dyne to suck her dusty toes after which she whipped him with her hair.

An eruption of lawn sprinklers sent actors and audience scurrying for cover through the mist and the rainbows, head and leaf baptized alike. An enraged Freya demanded the identity of the prankster who had dared to ruin her scene, but there was no one within twenty yards of the faucet but an unconscious drunk with a condom for a hat.

Objects continued to disclose for Perry an unnerving

shimmer even after the water had been turned off. Was this the herald of a lunacy the opening to which he had already observed in his viewfinder? He worried about fainting at an inopportune time.

"I feel funny," he complained to Freya. "I think there's drugs in the food."

Freya replied in the grand manner, "I serve no drug but that of love."

Elsie scrutinized him as if he were a particularly offensively dressed mannequin.

"Let's do it," Freya barked, like an honest-to-God American.

Banks of hard light mounted on tall poles had been repositioned about the picturesquely gnarled oak, a supporting character in its own right, high wattage carving an illuminated cave out of the solid opacity of the night, spectators gathered round like the crew at the site of an important archaeological dig, tense, subdued, primed for awe.

Freya called action! and Ula emerged from the darkness, clad in flimsy raiment of diaphanous veils she shed singly, artistically (Elvis dispensing stage scarves in Vegas the operative comparison), slithering across the floodlit space toward the tingling tree, more alive now than it had ever appeared in naked day, where Mr. Dyne, his scrawny arms strapped to a pair of Y-shaped branches, eyes girlishly aflutter, feigned to yield his hairless body into the ecstatic admixture of bliss and pain of which he fancied heaven was justly composed. The mesmerized crowd attended in lickerish silence, Freya squatting on a root barely out of camera range, the jeweled irises of several crouched cats glittering down from the upper limbs, the incense of grilled meat wafting lazily over all. Perry zoomed in for the close-up. The sight of Ula's virtuosic mouth working Mr. Dyne's floppy crank with an ardor even the jaded might term "indelicate" introduced a potent dose of skittering ambivalence into Perry's jeopardized systems. In accordance with the dictum: peer long enough into the camera and the camera will peer into you, he seemed to split into two distinct but identical organisms, sharing between them nonetheless, like yoked twins a common heart, one tattered shuttlecock of an ego being batted from this perceptual center to that in a brisk volley that left him confused as to which self was the original or indeed, whether such quaint concepts as "originality" were even valid, in both the ontological and epistemological senses. It was all Perry could do to keep the camera steady and aimed in the proper direction.

At the climactic moment Mr. Dyne tossed his moist head back against the ragged bark and emitted an scream so exaggerated, so cinematically feminine, onlookers stared about in bewilderment, uncertain whether to laugh, applaud, or rush to his aid. His dimpled chin dropped to his chest, lolled lifelessly to one side, and there was silence.

"Is he dead?" someone asked.

Perry focused in on Ula who gave the elided camera the startled doe gaze of one caught in a crime she had momentarily forgotten was illegal, the blankness persisting for only a beat before she flashed the loosest grin of the night, blew the lens a soulful kiss, and scampered nimbly for the house. Perry stopped tape. Mr. Dyne had not yet stirred, much of his audience, grown quite bored with his wooden impersonation, his rubber member, were already deep in the wholesome embrace of one another, naked duos, trios, quartets even, in all combos, distributed across the sloping lawn, heavily engaged in (insert favorite sexual practice), versatile

Freya striding anxiously amongst the fun, directing Perry's laggard camera from one novel clinch to the next, herself pursued by the twinge of melancholy (none must ever know) such a feast sometimes raised in her, the spectacle of the multitudes dying. Editing, however, was the great anodyne—there she could maintain the flow of arousal through time, her way of sticking it to death in the ass.

"The woman is an absolute witch," someone said.

"Triple X certainly," said someone else, "but is it politically correct?"

Perry at this point, incertitude as real as a disease to him, was stumbling around inside the notion that perhaps not everything he was beholding through his trusty camcorder was actually "out there." The last image he remembered framing as an objective fact was of a dignified gentleman in a Vandyke beard, latex gloves, and nothing else, hunched behind a juniper bush, furiously masturbating onto a slice of wheat bread.

Events assumed a hyperreal clarity.

He saw Satan himself, an electrical charcoal starter in each taloned fist, chasing a big-bottomed nymph into the garage. He saw, under a picnic table, Eric and Elsie, with artistic gravity, shaving one another's pubic hair. He saw Mr. Dyne raised from the dead and floating in bright radiance above the roof from where he tossed frozen pizzas to the starving flock. He saw Senator Wilcox running a slimy tongue into Ula's flushed ear.

He understood this was the vision of the mad, the prophets, where all is revealed as it is. He had been blessed.

OF LIGHTENING AND DISORDERED SOULS

DOUG RICE

Tell me.

Caddie lived herself within the walls of Doug thinking out loud the existence of his flesh. Who is there? You can talk. Out past the frontier I stood erect mixing with the laughter of all the snakes. Everywhere the snakes of Caddie crawled. Her hair alive in the pain. Constricting my attempts to move. Releasing my throat. Don't sit under the apple tree with nobody else. But the devil down from the heavens above and Torgov trying to fly like a bat. Desiring. For a swollen belly. For languages. For blood. Burning her name. My name is Doug and I have not lived inside here for a very long time. My name is Caddie but she is just a practice at odds with saying, "That's not it." Caddie retouched herself. Me. At odds with what existed before her very eyes, Doug goes off in all directions unknowing herself. Experiencing pleasure almost everywhere across the lands of her body Doug was too terrified to move. But the pleasures kept spreading across his body. Without. And languages how can I say this and Caddie but she could say.

Caddie, possessed by a state of reckless bliss, sat down at my body and began fingering my flesh with her teeth. Losing her tongue in ways infinitely different from those ways that she had been taught to dread. In the past, in my heart, in what I have done. My body squirmed under her flesh of my flesh in the unity of parted tongues as of that fire filled with those holy spirits trapped by grandma Mugwump. Speaking not in the words that made me. Whose story can you tell now? Are you not. All these voices that are speaking ancestors are you. Echoes bouncing, caressing. Tomorrow and tomorrow. And how has Caddie spoken in each of the languages in which she was born? Come. Caddie, the soul's most welcome guest, toils with the snake of our peace in passion. But her fingers knew the snakes in my souls and my words spoken against her cunt. Did you hear this. Me now. How could she expect me to see any of this.

There came a sound from the stove. Grandma had, clang, dropped a ladle on the floor. Where we were sitting, the violent wind of Grandma's speaking—into that time passing off the clock out of the window into the garden—the wonderful works of Poppy Torgov filled our memories. You never listen closely enough Doug. Did you. Pouring out the story, Grandma sprinkled some spices over the soup. The steam rising out of the pot. Grandma in foggy glasses stirring. Not seeing, speaking.

"Before Poppy Torgov began working the railroad, he spent most of his time running around the backroads following the lazy streets of an odd job circuit. One summer, living in the choked, humid atmosphere of Philadelphia, he started his own business. He opened a clinic and served the city as a professed doctor of cellulite removal. Women, from near and far, flocked to him. He also used ads to search out men troubled by varicose veins. It was rare, back then, for a doctor to have two specialties and Andreas soon became the host of the town."

"People, especially women, sent him photos of themselves from across the seas hoping there was something he could offer. By carefully studying a videotape, he had learned a trick from Meryl Streep about different ways to alter x-rays. So he adopted this trick as his own and used it to alter the photographs these women mailed to him. Having corrected their photographs, he charged them by the pound ($12.50/lb.) for the cellulite that he told them he would soon be removing. There was no pain involved in any of these procedures.

"Removing varicose veins, on the other hand, almost always proved to be lethal. The weapons were always too hard, too sharp and diseased. Only a few of Poppy's patients were ever able to survive. Those with large varicose veins on their calves had the best chance for survival, but they usually ended up losing the motor movement of at least one of their feet. Without fail, Poppy did always manage to kill those who had varicose veins on their penises and most of the time he also lost those with varicose veins along the insides of their thighs. And even though each operation was successful, he was soon being called a butcher by members of the medical community.

"Poppy just got carried away, caught up in the moment, when he undid men's veins. The incision was simple enough but complications arose when the men could not contain their blood. Poppy tried to teach them to re-direct their blood, to make it flow dispersed through other parts of their bodies, re-route it into other veins. But the heat involved in this delicate operation always just seemed to be a bit too much."

"A series of malpractice suits have been filed against Dr. Andreas Torgov. Patients believe he has been using mirrors to remove cellulite from their thighs. The most serious complaints came from a group of women who claimed that he simply doctored photographs and never once laid a hand on them. Other advances in modern medicine are also under attack in Germany. There, researchers have developed an odorless gas capable of numbing the nervous system in such a severe way that the people forget they are human. In this way, doctors are able to continue to work on their living tissue without needing to worry.

"I quit my past as soon as I heard Andreas speaking to me. I gave up my body to the rag and bone shop in the basement of the prison a few days after Andreas taught me how to eat blood. We were cellmates. Incarcerated. I had been arrested for loitering with a sinister intention outside one of the new shopping malls in the suburbs of Philly. He told me I would become the perfect woman for him. I had to first learn to eat women, to consume the spaces that they occupied. He taught me the blood of women. He taught me to watch for the way the white light of the moon fell onto their bodies, over their flesh. If the moon flickered, causing a kind of dance on their shoulders, then I should feed on that woman.

"Andreas made himself into the first time I had ever been with another man. Careful they might hear us. First he taught me the manners of loving another man, the turns of the body, the ways that men's bodies travelled down always down toward the earth. And then, out of nowhere, he made my cock disappear for good. We cornered a female prison guard and I ended my life. I took on the image Andreas had built out of the guard's blood for me and fled, resigning my position at the prison."

Caddie probed me.

"On the outside I got a job as a woman. Listening. The dishes aren't done. Hearing all of those men confessing their needs to sin. Beat me my mommy. Are you white? Want to be my sister? You wish you were here. I wish I was you with that great nig cock of yours. If a microwave is for me, why can't I just have one? Right now. Such a monster, so big. My sister. That one over there. I've got something here for you. That can't really be one. I'm your mommy and you've been so naughty. Not a real one. Tell me how ya'd like to suck it. I'm just exhausted. You want it inside you. Tell me you used to me a man. I've had such a bad day at work. I know where you live. Listen to you calling me. A faggot. A whore. A bastard. My god. 'Night mother. Quit cutting out those goddamn coupons. Just wait until I get my hands on you. Who's that calling you now? Is that your hand. You make me hard. Wet I mean."

—See Dick run?

—Hear Jane walk?

—Run Dick run.

—Whisper Jane whisper.

"That first night out of jail I started waiting for Poppy to finish serving his term. Out for good behavior. Soon. I prayed back the loneliness. I played, excessively, with my clit. Anything but that. I want to feel your whip. I prowled the highways. Stalked the streets of one-night cheap hotels that I had found in the library. Waiting. Until I began to see my cock re-appearing out of the nowhere. As I stood in the mirror, at the mirror, looking back my breasts disappearing. Road trip to Scranton. Or was it Susquehanna.

"I was so dangerously young way back then before turning into a menace, before meeting Poppy. Such a boy. Koufax tossing no-hitters and Wills leading off, stealing second every single time. Squinting eyes, living inside the wind-up. Desiring second. Wanting. Then. Bam. Gone. Safe. I think that what I liked most about Maury Wills was his skin. On TV it was so soft. And that smile. He was always so happy having just stolen second. How could he possibly slide into second without ever scraping his knees, his elbows? It was as if God was down there with him. Watching out for that beautiful skin. Stretching out that lead on second. Paranoing the pitcher. Marichael. Gibson. Throwing fast and hard. Trying not to let Wills run loose. Davis at bat, the other Davis on deck. I died waiting all through the winter for opening day. Thought I would be a ballplayer someday, shagging flies, chasing women. Getting a tan. Laughing with the other boys of summer. Never dying. April sweet April, month of dreams.

"Now look at me."

Grandma Mugwump stood stirring. She could never play baseball now. The knees are the first to go. Could never round the bags again.

Not with eyes. Caddie I am sorry if I have offended you. I looked up into the language of Caddie standing over me, so strong. Wanting. To feel her take her pleasure out of my body with her desires. Stolen from some other God, that one, not here. Made Doug her soldier.

—Forgive me Father for I have sinned. It has been, I mean, this is my first confession. I haven't done anything that we've talked about. I would like to be God.

"I'm not telling a priest that."

Talking, Caddie showed me nothing there. And said to me, "Do you think there is really nothing there?"

Her and Grandma Nothing There Either Mugwump. My

kind of life.

"The problem is," Caddie was saying there in the words, "Doug just can't see everything there all at once." I was at her feet.

Caddie can't possibly expect Doug to tell a priest that. My tongue. Not with your tongue. And my cock. Caddie. Which one is caddie?

—In the name of the Father and of the Son and there I am saying it.

—Forgive me Father for I have sinned. It has been two weeks since my last confession. I have a list here.

Alert and secret and without shame, Grandma Mugwump moved away from the stove. She stood there behind Caddie with her hands on Caddie's shoulders. Her body had grown so hard, almost unknown. I am still. Watching her, she touches, it was like I was somehow looking at myself and my own way for touching Caddie came out of Grandma's eyes. Grandma turned at me. She looked and I felt she was making me want to touch Caddie. But Grandma just started talking again. My tongue danced silently outside of my body. I am not doing. Caddie's body, beautiful and small, moved with each word. And Caddie touching Grandma back now and me sitting here just listening in, trying to overhear.

"By the time that Poppy finally got out of jail, my body had somehow escaped out of me. My hair stood on end, erect, laughing at me. Snakes turned against my womb. Hustling with the whores on the corner of Columbia and Broad. Scenes passing from a million years, sliding down onto my knees praying. God in the hour of our deaths and taking him into me. But down there, not down there. My cock grew. Throbbing and stinging my cunt. Switching. God let my breasts suffer again through his touch. His fingers and.

God touching out of the skies my breasts caving and him saying, trying to say, 'You faggot.' Thinking I was a man, am a man, he tore at my nipples as my breasts disappeared against the old rail station. My back. Cold, cold but is this summer time. I can love you for what I am. Let me. Screaming to his friends. Praying only his voice would come back. But no. Out of the streets came. Which way the wind blows. His friends. Faggot I stood on my knees. My cock destroyed out of, destroyed into my cunt. Gone. I ate. A feast of all these men, young and hard, into me. I swallowed their cocks into my cock and lost my and, couldn't talk, but slipped into this used to be that was me then me now. Thought that was me and I recognized this is me as my cock grew out of me. My body collapsed and I became no longer not a woman and my cock ached to fuck strong."

—Forgive me Father, for I am sinning.

"That night, bloodied chin, I slept. Tasted, eaten, so many bodies and bloods. Remembering if this was what I am. Carried by a woman. Thinking back when this was tomorrow. Yesterday I sat at my window flesh for Juliet if she. And she. Her pain on my flesh. No, not that. But before and I was watching and my mother said, 'Go outside.' And I knew no that I could not but I did and there I played."

—Forgive me Father, for I have sinned. It has been two weeks, a little longer, since my last confession. Caddie said, told me.

"When I was a young boy I remember Lindsey across the street. 'Stay away from her.' And Susie. Older Susie. She drove a car. She was older and me riding my bike with Andrew up and down the street. Singing. Get out of my life. Young girl. But she was older. After the rain. And Susie out of her door to her car parked on the side of the street. Wearing boots, so high and so white, and hip hugging shorts and not knowing exactly what I hoped to see. Praying. Not even knowing for sure if I actually wanted to see. Then she drove away. And Andrew and me racing on our bikes to ride over the dry spot. My heart racing against me, my bike against Andrew. Racing. Sometimes being the first to ride over the dry spot that Susie's car had left on the road.

"Sometimes not."

—You can't wear that son.

Listen to me. Dammit Doug, don't break that.

"Poppy found me his first night out of jail. In the park. Romance everywhere. Poppy looking out into my eyes and telling me. How he wanted to have children. How I could be a woman again and my cock getting hard just thinking about it. Poppy's hand warming my thigh and him saying and me seeing no one looking. And we yes our lips. Out of the dark a flash."

"Only four hours after being released from jail, Andreas Torgov is once again in custody for having apparently violated the terms of his parole.

"A photographer, covering the Museum Park area, accidentally discovered Mr. Torgov once again practicing his controversial and illegal ideas about the removal of varicose veins from other men. Photographed, in what can only be called a moment or two of sheer violent struggle with another man, Torgov reportedly forced his mouth onto the lips of the other man. Torgov's subject, operating under what we can only assume is some sort of alias—Mugwump, had no evidence of varicose veins anywhere on his body.

"Mugwump could not say anything when responding to all of the questions. He seemed to be rather frightened, kind of trapped in our world not understanding. Torgov, on the other hand, said he was caught off guard and was surprised to be told that Mugwump is a man. According to Torgov, 'Mugwump reminded me so much of a woman I had known in high school that I just figured that she was a woman. I did not know that Mugwump was a man because we were only kissing. It did not go any further than that.'

"When the police asked if Mugwump's name did not make him suspicious, Torgov replied that he did not know her name at the time. If he had, Torgov said in his defense, 'I probably would not have kissed him to begin with.' Feeling that everyone involved had been through enough, Torgov decided not to file counter-charges against Mugwump. And that's the world in a minute. In other news"

—Forgive me Father, for I have, for I want to. I would like to be a nun. When I grow up I want to be a nun.

—There is no sin in wanting to be a teacher when you grow up my son.

Sometimes Caddie, these words they become so easy just to believe in. And I look out against myself and think sometimes Caddie these words are just so easy to believe.

"Poppy rushed into my arms. A man is walking alone and a woman cries at home. But we were inside and Poppy and I were together making love. Hard. And then he went out to. And he brought her home. And out of the fluttering screaming white feathers I again became this woman that I wanted.

"And Poppy said yes now we can have the child that we wanted, always. And yes I said again yes now that I had the body that we needed. And children could become something that my body could now have. And we decided, there and then, that there was nothing wrong, not really, with Poppy being a man and me being a woman. And that is the way it could be then."

The Elements of Style
Painstakingly translated by Derek Pell
With Index

THE

ELEMENTS

OF

Style

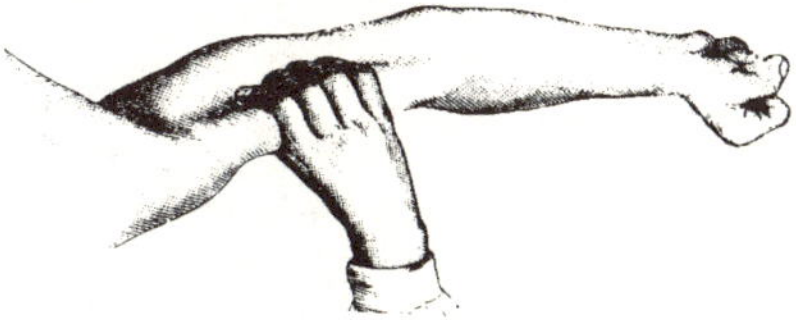

BY

The Marquis de Sade

With Revisions, an Introduction, and a Chapter on Writhing

BY

E. B. WHIPE

THIRD EDITION

Painstakingly translated by Derek Pell

"Sade...[his] pornographic messages are embodied in sentences so pure they might be used as grammatical models."

—Roland Barthes
The Pleasure of the Text

a c h e k n o w l e d g e m e n t

This book is for Peter Gambaccini

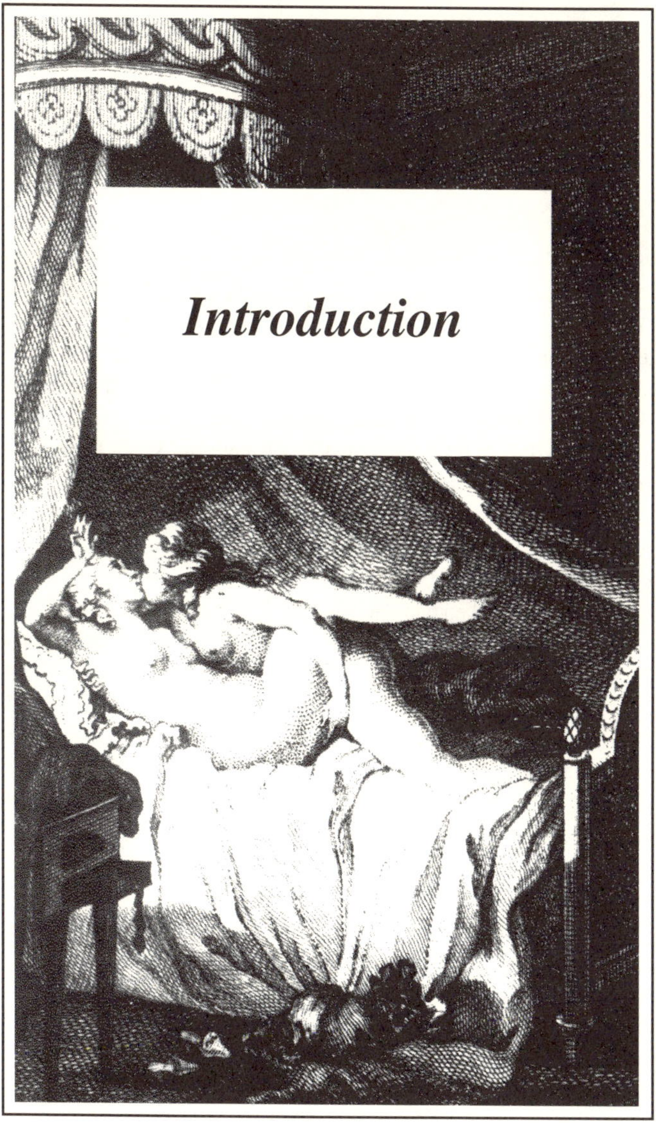

Introduction

INTRODUCTION

Ten days prior to the deforming of the Bastille, and long before I had learned to read or write, the Marquis de Sade* went on a sabbatical to Charenton** lunatic asylum. There, despite inadequate accomodations, he began writing a textbook called *Le Eléments de Style*. The manuscript soon became known among the inmate population as "120 Pages de Ennui"—a title prompted less by the author's worthy message than the prose by which he imparted it. Indeed, the work was marred by pedantic repetitions and insufferably bad puns. Such sins might easily have been overlooked had Sade chosen to include illustrations.

In 1957, while I was browsing in an adult bookshop on the Champs Elysées, I stumbled upon the first (and only) edition of *Le Eléments de Style*, bound in a fellow inmate's flesh***. I immediately expressed my disdain at the fact that the slender volume contained not a single picture. The proprietor simply shrugged and spat at my feet. Still, I detected among the book's yellowed pages rich deposits of gold amid the dust and rhetorical debris. It was, I realized, the Marquis de Sade's *parvum opus*, his attempt to cut the French student body down to size and to instill a sense of badly needed discipline. Of course, at the time of publication [1795], the work was considered too tyranical in nature for use in reform schools. Yet there was no denying that his little book

---

* France's foremost adult educator and disciplinarian

** Recently renamed the Sheraton Inn for the Criminally Out of It.

*** Alphonse Buckram

was a masterpiece. Sade himself had apparently hung the tag "little" on the volume, as he often referred to it sardonically and with secret pride by saying, "Walk softly and carry my *little* book." He always gave the word "little" a special twist while glancing down at his crotch.

What struck me then (and I still have the scars to prove it) was the realization that the American academic community could greatly benefit from the Master's instructions, if only the peculiar prose could be rendered into English without all those silly little accent marks. I decided to take a crack at it, to edit the work and, in a way, make it my own. Hell, "Sade is dead," as Sartre once said, and I felt entitled to tamper with his text, to whip it into shape, so to speak.

The Marquis de Sade was a memorable man, friendly, funny, and tempermental. Under the remembered sting of his kindly lash, I have tried to follow in his footnotes, to profit from his words with each new printing of *Le Eléments de Style.* In the English classes of today, this "little book" is surrounded by longer, harder, better endowed tomes. Perhaps this textbook has become something of a curiosity, for even though few students heed its advice they certainly study the pictures. For me, this "little" book maintains its original stature, standing erect, resolute, and assured. I still find Sade's cruel wisdom a comfort, his rancor a delight, and his penetrating insight into right-and-wrong a blessing. His last words linger on:

"Education *smarts*..."

Elementary Principles of Composition

Omit needless words.

Madame de Gernande, aged nineteen and a half, had the most lovely, the most noble, the most majestic figure one could hope to see, not one of her gestures, not a single movement was without gracefulness, not one of her glances lacked depth of sentiment: nothing could equal the expression of her eyes, which were a beautiful dark brown although her hair was blond; but a certain languor, a lassitude entailed by her misfortunes, dimmed their *éclat*, and thereby rendered them a thousand times more interesting; her skin was very fair, her hair very rich; her mouth was very small, perhaps too small, and I was little surprised to find this defect in her: 'twas a pretty rose not yet in full bloom; but teeth so white...lips of a vermillion...one might have said Love had colored them with tints borrowed from the goddess of flowers; her nose was aquiline, straight, delicately modeled; upon her brow curved two ebony eyebrows; a perfectly lovely chin; a visage, in one word, of the finest oval shape, over whose entirety reigned a kind of attractiveness, a naïveté, an openness which might well have made one take this adorable face for an angelic rather than mortal physiognomy. Her arms, her breasts, her flanks were of a splendor...of a round fullness fit to serve as models to an artist; a black silken fleece covered her *mons veneris*, which was sustained by two superbly cast thighs; and what astonished me was that, despite the slenderness of the Countess' figure, despite her sufferings, nothing had impaired the firm quality of her flesh: her round, plump buttocks were as smooth, as ripe, as firm as if her figure were heavier and as if she had always dwelled in the depths of happiness. However, frightful traces of her husband's libertinage were scattered thickly about; but, I repeat, nothing spoiled, nothing damaged...the very image of a beautiful lily upon which the honeybee has inflicted some scratches. To so many gifts Madame de

Gernande added a gentle nature, a romantic and tender mind, a heart of such sensibility!

The paragraph above may be reduced to the following sentence:

Madame de Gernande was a piece of ass.

Avoid a succession of loose sentences.

Make an unbreakable habit of daintiness. Always start the day with clean underwear and hosiery. If you haven't time or strength to iron crepe slips and panties, wear the knit variety that needs no pressing. But don't get an "extra day's wear" from you lingerie. There is little difference between *dirty* underwear and *slightly soiled* underwear.

Apart from its triteness and emptiness, the paragraph above is bad because of the structure of its sentences, with their mechanical symmetry and singsong. Compare these sentences

"Wait one moment," says the berserk monk, "I want to flog simultaneously the most beautiful of behinds and the softest of breasts." He leaves me on my knees and, bringing Armande toward me, makes her stand facing me with her legs spread, in such a way that my mouth touches her womb and my breasts are exposed between her thighs and below her behind; by this means the monk has what he wants before him: Armande's buttocks and my titties in close proximity: furiously he beats them both, but my companion, in order to spare me blows which are becoming far more dangerous for me than for her, has the goodness to lower herself and thus shield me by receiving upon her own person the lashes that would inevitably have wounded me.

Use definite, specific, concrete language.

These groupings were frequent; for when a monk indulged in whatever form of pleasure, all the girls regularly surrounded him in order to fire all his parts' sensations, that voluptuousness might, if one may be forgiven the expression, more surely penetrate into him through every pore.

Place the emphatic words of a sentence at the end.

The proper place in the sentence for the word or group of words that the writer desires to make most prominent is usually the end.

...You, Eugénie, bestow two good smacks upon Madame your Mother and as soon as she gains the threshold, help her cross it with a few lusty kicks aimed at her ass.

RULE.—Be careful to read the last word in a full and loud tone.

A Few Matters of Form

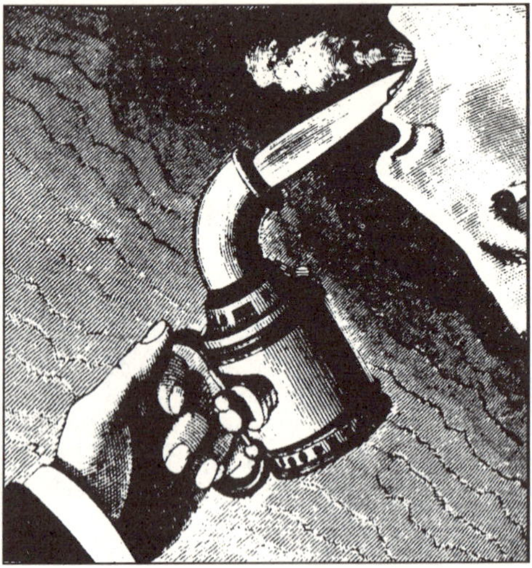

Numerals. Do not spell out dates or other serial numbers. Write them in figures or in Roman notation, as may be appropriate.

> *October 29*—By order of the King, the Marquis de Sade is committed to Vincennes fortress for excesses committed in a brothel which he has been frequenting for a month.
>
> *Les 120 Journées de Sodome*
>
> 1. As regards the laws of Nature only, is this act really criminal?

Quotations. When a quotation is followed by an attributive phrase, the comma is enclosed within the quotation marks.

> "On your knees," the monk said to me, "I am going to whip your titties."

Titles.

Les Journées de Florbelle, ou la Nature dévoilée, suivies des Mémoires de l'abbé de Modose et des Aventures d'Emilie de Volnange servant de preuves aux assertions, ouvrage orné de deux cents gravures.

For the titles of literary works, a good rule of thumb is: a title should never exceed the length of the author's penis.

Colloquialisms. If you use a colloquialism or a slang word or phrase, simply use it; do not draw attention to it by enclosing it in quotation marks.

"I'm not that kind of girl"

Exclamations. Do not attempt to emphasize simple statements by using a mark of exclamation.

> MADAME DE SAINT-ANGE—I engaged fifteen men, alone; in twenty-four hours, I was ninety times fucked!
>
> What a marvelous invention!

The exclamation mark is to be reserved for use after true exclamations or commands.

> —Oh, please, dear friend, allow me to frig this splendid member!
>
> "Oh, Great God!" I exclaimed, casting myself at Roland

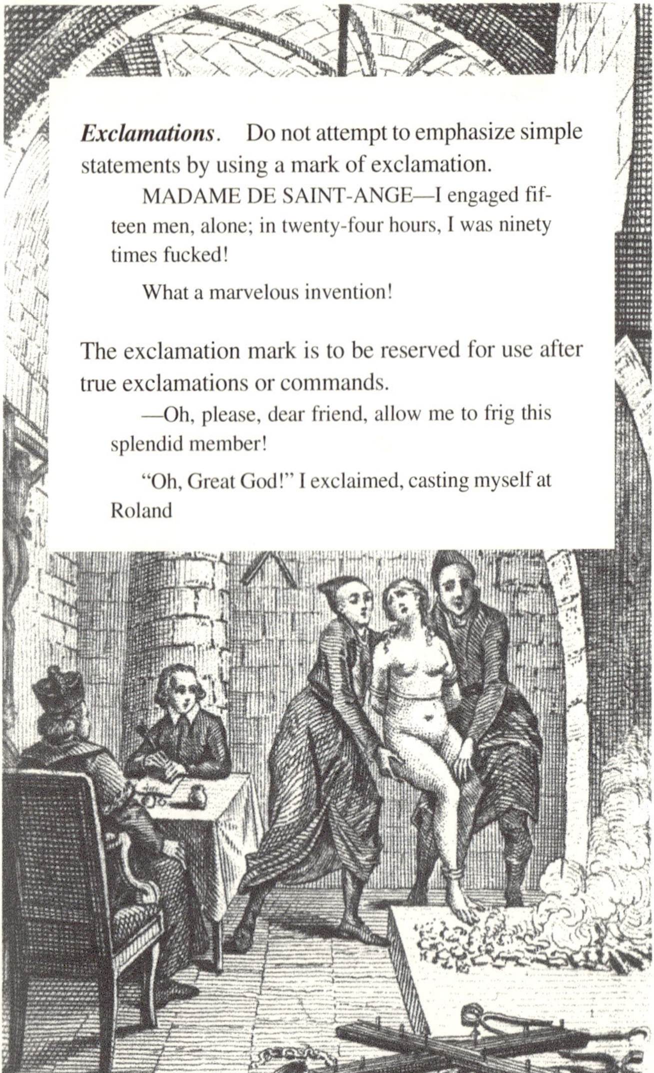

Words and Expressions Commonly Misused

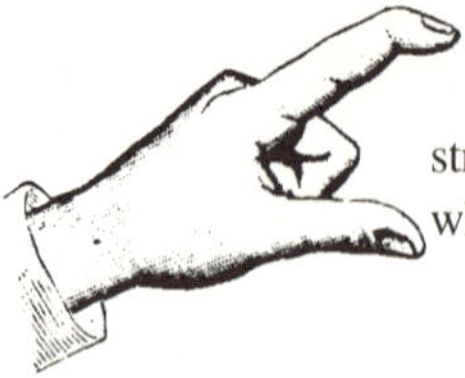

Enormity. Use only in the sense "monstrous wickedness." Misleading, if not wrong, when used to express bigness.

Vir•tu•ous. Might mean "objectionable," "disconcerting," "distasteful." Select instead a word whose meaning is clear: frig•id

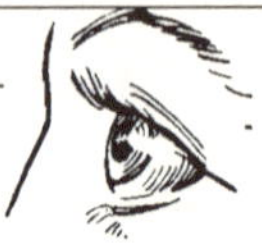

To flog a dead horse. Means one thing when applied to men, another when applied to horses.

Bugger. Often used because to the writer it sounds more impressive than **bumming**. Such usage is not incorrect but is to be guarded against.

Sock it to me. Literally, "embrace."

Cattle prod. A clumsy, pretentious device, much in vogue. Find a better way.

Dead meat. Sometimes means "**blind date**."

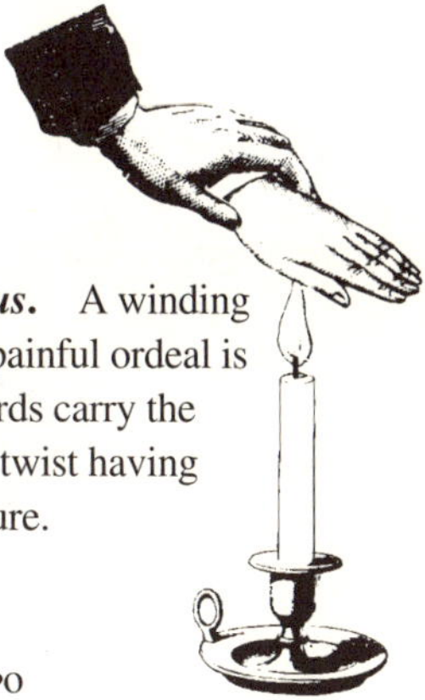

Tortuous. Torturous. A winding road is *tortuous*, a painful ordeal is *torturous*. Both words carry the idea of "twist," the twist having been a form of torture.

Sociopathic personality. See Ro•me•o

God created a perfect world …A bad beginning for a sentence. If you feel you are possessed of the truth, better discard it entirely.

Student body. Nine times out of ten a needless and awkward expression, meaning no more than

cadaver

To beat about the bush. A cliché, and a fuzzy one.

Overkill. A word with many meanings.

Vice squad. These words may usually be omitted with advantage.

Invitation. See *put the screws on*

Aphrodisiac. See **mercy killing**

Split infinitive. There is a precedent from the fourteenth century down for interposing an adverb between *to* and the infinitive it governs, but the construction should be avoided unless the writer wishes to place unusual stress on the adverb.

to diligently *Whip*   to *Whip* diligently

To lick into shape. Use it sparingly. Save it for specific application.

Finishing school. Often unnecessary.

Dead. Often an adjective of last resort. It's in the dictionary, but that doesn't mean you have to use it.

An Approach to Style

(With a List of Reminders)

Write in a way that comes naturally.

Write in a way that comes easily and naturally to you, using words and phrases that come readily to hand.

> "And now spread them, Madame," the Count said brutally.

Do not affect a breezy manner.

The volume of writing is enormous, these days, and much of it has a sort of windiness about it, almost as though the author were in a state of euphoria.

> "The impure monk uninterruptedly occupied with me in like fashion, then tells me to give the largest possible vent to whatever winds may be hovering in my bowels, and these I am to direct into his mouth."

The breezy style is often the work of an egocentric, the person who imagines that everything that pops into his head is of general interest.

Make sure the reader knows who is speaking.

Dialogue is a total loss unless you indicate who the speaker is. In long dialogue passages containing no attributives, the reader may become lost and be compelled to go back and reread in order to puzzle the thing out.

> "But the man you describe is a monster."
> "The man I describe is in tune with Nature."
> "He is a savage beast."

"'Tis impossible."
"Impossible?"
"Absolutely."
"Could you explain…"
"No, that's our secret."

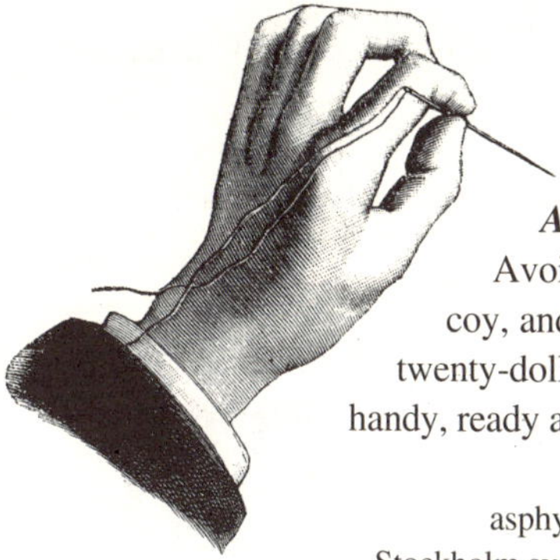

Avoid fancy words.

Avoid the elaborate, the pretentious, the coy, and the cute. Do not be tempted by a twenty-dollar word when there is a ten-center handy, ready and able.

asphyxiation	assault and battery
Stockholm syndrome	poetic punishment
victimological	bludgeon
crime passionnel	*post mortem*
guillotine	garrote
pornokitsch	sadomasochist

Be clear.

worst, and that in the very thick of disorder and corruption, all of what mankind calls happiness may shed itself bountifully upon life; but let this cruel and fatal truth cause no alarm; let honest folk be no more seriously tormented by the example we are going to present of disaster everywhere dogging the heels of Virtue; this criminal felicity is deceiving, it is seeming only; independently of the punishment most certainly reserved by Providence for those whom success in crime has seduced, do they not nourish in the depths of their soul a worm which unceasingly gnaws, prevents them from finding joy in these fictive gleams of meretricious well-being, and, instead of delights, leaves naught in their soul but the rending memory of the crimes which have led them to where they are?

Clarity, clarity, clarity. When you become hopelessly mired in a sentence, it is best to start fresh:

To these horrors Madame de Lorsange added three or four infanticides.

Avoid the use of qualifiers.

Rather, very, little, pretty—these are the leeches that infest the pond of prose, sucking the blood of words.

"Upon the first day of every month each monk adopts a girl who must serve a term as his servant and as the target of his very shameful desires."

Use a dash to set off an abrupt break or interruption.

"Thérèse," he says, "you are going to suffer cruelly"—he had no need to tell me so, for his eyes declared it.

Prefer the standard to the offbeat.

The young writer will be drawn at every turn toward eccentricities in language. He will hear the beat of new vocabularies, the exciting rhythms.

> A third girl, kneeling before him, begins to excite him with her hands, and a fourth, completely naked, with her fingers indicates where he must strike my body. Gradually, this girl begins to arouse me and what she does to me Antonin does as well, with both his hands, to two other girls on his left and right.

Use orthodox spelling.

In ordinary composition, use orthodox spelling. Do not write Mame for maim.

Avoid foreign languages.

The writer will occasionally find it convenient or necessary to borrow from other languages. Some writers, however, from sheer exuberance or a desire to show off, sprinkle their work liberally with foreign expressions, with no regard for the reader's comfort.

Siegeszug wird. Bis jetzt druckten beispielsweise die Türken den sonderbaren Schnörkel اوطوموبيل hin oder schrieben den noch seltsameren Schnörkel اوطوموبل hin, wenn sie den Begriff „Automobil" versinnbildlichen wollten.

Write in English

Do not inject opinion.

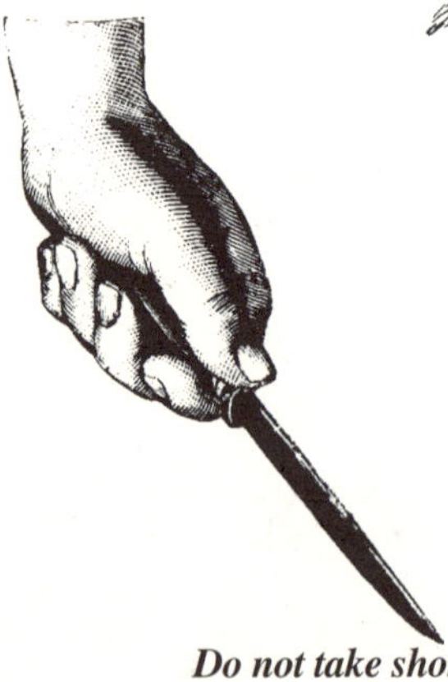

Do not take shortcuts at the cost of clarity.

Do not explain too much.

Two nights later, I slept with Jérôme; I will not describe his horrors to you; they were still more terrifying.

It is seldom advisable to tell all.

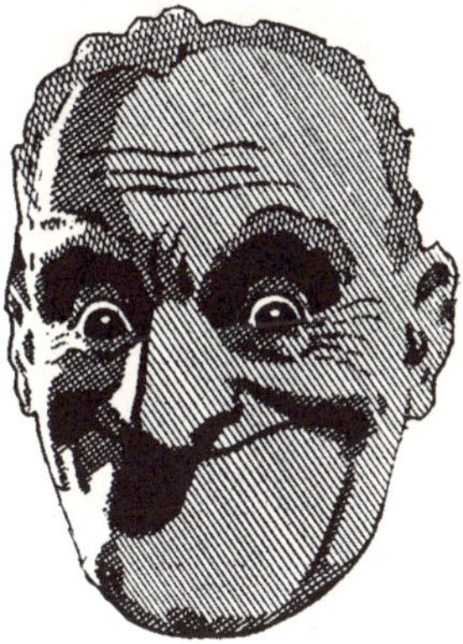

D. A. F. de Sade.

Sade
and
WHIPE
Index

ONCE UPON A REAL WOMAN

EURUDICE

Ever since her cunt ran away, Ela's loft, replete with glass and bones, repulses Ela. She needs the energy of a crowd, she craves a quick charge.

She covers her lips under a black silk "purdah" like a Rajput maharani, and like the night she descends on the city in a little red lace dress.

A towering hulky woman in blue velvet overalls, with breasts bulky and hard like grapefruit, with curly red hair a la Cher and with no fingers past her crumpled knuckles, grasps Ela's loose unsuspecting hand with the gesture of a medieval knight and calls her: "Sister!"

At once Ela drops her silver head face down into the stranger's stupendous cleavage and wonders if she could actually manage to decuntate such a huge woman.

As the fingerless lesbian spontaneously hugs Ela, Ela disappears inside that ingeniously comfortable chest.

The lesbian's breasts smell like cayenne pepper, old seaweed and moist scouring pads. She wears nothing under her ample overalls, so that Ela can see, from where she lies buried, only the big off-white pores and stretch marks of those flabby long tits. Ela sneezes.

The lesbian invites her to her house, and specifies: "I hate talking about myself, believe it or not. I lie all the time. I have two kids. They are nice accessories. I don't breastfeed. I prefer having my bottom spanked. I am casual but avid about sex. I am not oversexed. Have you always been an exception?"

Ela: "I too am a congenital liar. It is true. I never say the truth." She speaks fast and breathlessly, so that her listener is overtaken by the terror that Ela will suffocate at any minute, give out three tiny spasms and expire. Her voice purls and scintillates, innocent of all sense.

The big lesbian booms: "You have the voice of a soothsayer."

Ela clarifies: "A seafarer?"

The big lesbian blares: "Call me any names you see fit."

Ela hums: "A rose by any other name..."

The big lesbian, alias Proserpina, hollers: "You may call me a symptom of nature. I will pass."

Ela lies happily cuddled in the grandiose peppery tits and senses a vague déjà-vu that washes her in a wave of sleepiness.

The big lesbian, a.k.a. Desdemona: "These days, our witches carry themselves as queens. They dress elegantly and raid our cities, looking so beautiful that no one notices their gold blank eyes. They quietly steal our children from the candy aisle while lightning strikes outside one afternoon and a tired cashier makes a punching error. These rebels teach our youth to love horror: the horror of a belly that thinks, of an eye that reflects rather than sees, of an ear that absorbs like a sponge of memory. They swallow our children whole with the bones like game birds, after they have danced with them in the light of old desires. Don't be fooled by these women's fresh tormenting smells and painted shy smiles. They have come to eat our sons who are beautiful like daughters and our daughters who are strong like sons."

Ela is lulled by the lesbian's fairytale. She thoughtlessly follows the big fingerless lesbian home.

The enormous unwieldy breasts, heavy like exotic giant mushrooms, bounce and slap Ela's tender face as she walks backwards with tiny uncertain steps, still hiding between their mounds. The two women make a striking couple.

Ela whispers: "I draw pleasure from sweet and wild fucks that are born away from men; I like coming in the mirror."

Soon after, Ela lies on her back on a blue waterbed that swirls and swells and swishes and caves in, like a sex-doll's rubber mouth opening up to swallow her.

The room is submerged in '50s memorabilia: Coca-Cola bottles, long car fenders, red Dorothy slippers, a *Cabaret* black hat, a pink juke-box, a yellow soda-counter, an original *Gone with the Wind* poster.

A tremendous strapping naked Aspasia pounces through the bedroom door: gone are the overalls, the high heels, the bobbed perm, the lipstick and the tight girdle that made her look human.

This Hecuba bursts in with her red hair pulled back, her puffy cheeks flushed, biting her bloated lips, looking like:

a. hungry dishevelled seamstress turned Jacobite rebel who is breaking into the Bastille and then haunting Marat's home;

b. a hefty Spanish butcheress who has just killed her husband in a moment of bad temper;

c. a mean chunky Nazi colonel in charge of a concentration camp with a fondness for heavy sweets and thin cocks;

d. a female Sumo wrestler;

e. the robust runner in Picasso's "The Race."

Big-footed, soft-assed, flop-titted, thick-waisted, red-faced, bulb-eyed, rough-hewn, Beiruta holds out her fleshy arms to Ela and makes it clear that she doesn't care what happens.

Ela dives freely into that mountainous lumpy softness and sucks it at random.

But it is Ela who is being sucked into endless freckled folds and sweaty creases and fleshy canyons, like in the tentacles of a giant squid, or into the mouth of a mammoth clam. Ela feels the various parts of her body crumpled up, spread out, warped, separated, and lost to her forever.

Only an elfin foot here or a narrow shoulder there spills out of the ample thumping female mass and indicates Ela's drowning presence on the squirming waterbed.

Hilda is endowed with the fattest longest clit Ela has ever seen, easily the largest in the world. A consummate mighty clit that fills Ela's field of vision and overflows beyond it.

Wanda's clit, larger than a homemade sausage, is in fact too big for Ela's tight mouth. It resembles a towering taut juicy cactus the color of an eggplant, twice the size of Ela's pinkie.

As Ela bravely faces that quivering red monster, she wonders how she can ever affect the nerve centers buried inside it. She spends the next hour yanking at it, whacking it, biting it, chewing it, pinching it, kneading it, slapping it, spanking it, stretching it, twisting it, scratching it, hoping to pass sensation through all that rugged muscle and fat.

It probably owes its awesome dimensions to countless such hours of fingering and pulling, Ela thinks admiringly.

When at long last Cassandra yelps inhumanly like a fatally wounded tigress, as if someone is presently piercing her heart on a sharpened spit and roasting it, Ela wipes her brow and falls exhausted on the red carpeted floor with the image of that purple demanding clit indelibly engraved in her mind.

But she has no time to rest.

Immediately after, the Great Barbarella lifts Ela up in her arms like a new bride and carries her to the nearby bathroom.

As she is being dropped in a single motion into a brimming steaming bathtub, Ela quickly notices a peach Laura Ashley wallpaper, a Francis Bacon on the moist wall, *9 ½ Weeks* blinds on the window and many dozens of herbal soaps, lotions and Body Shop creams all around Imelda's bathroom.

Next Ela notices that Hedda's brawny arms rival her swollen face in duskiness and that her eyes are slits. Mata flops herself on a nearby stool with her massive thighs wide open, rewarding Ela with a continued frontal viewing of her powerhouse-clit and of the sparse stringy red pubic hairs on her purple labia.

Like a mythic laundress, Leona employs her mighty forearms, her vast shoulders and colossal swinging breasts to clean Ela. Her gnarled stubs clasp a dozen bristly brushes expertly. She scrubs Ela with loofahs and oils until Ela, submerged in burning lather, cannot breathe through the suds that choke her mouth and nostrils, and her skin is white silk thinner than a newborn's.

Thelma, looking porky, happy and out of breath, asks: "Do you love Kant?" Then she sighs: "With a bar of soap in hand, a disinterested spectator would also wonder: could life be art?" Ela gasps, rumpled and giddy.

Zsa Zsa: "Sex is our only means of communication. Women have a clit in place of a heart. That's why we fall in love so easily."

Ela, regaining her breath: "I don't need to be loved. Au

contraire: I need to be received cordially and discreetly and asked for only my good manners in return. A calm acceptance suits me best, but I always receive passion instead."

Charlotta, lifting Ela once again: "Would you be offended if I confessed that right before we met I was having a turbulent love affair with a monkey? She liked to mince words."

Ela, in mid-air: "Who? Max?"

Sandra, confidentially to Ela in her arms: "No. Cubby Hole."

Ela, also intimately: "Earlier, as I laughingly poked your breasts with the points of my manicured nails, your resilient heavy flesh repelled my hands and a dull pain still lingers in my fingertips. I am at a loss as to what to do with my hand."

Renata, carrying Ela like a kitten: "From now on I'll be your bodyguard. When I hold you, I can't be sure I am holding you." Her heavy voice booms too shrill to reflect any feeling.

Ela: "Intense sorrows should bring special magic powers with them. I am in despair over the poverty of human emotions."

Vanna, a smile spreading across her huge face: "When the ghost of death haunts our every step, we can only create the world inside our home. My kitchen can serve a small hotel. My stereo is concert quality. I own every appliance I can find. Machines make me feel loved." The monotone of her unfocused voice grows threatening, developing into a downpour, and Ela feels the first drops of saliva on her forehead.

Ela: "I've never been comfortable myself. If I lived like Fellini in a Cinecitta of my own where I could create huge ships and startling towns out of papier mâché, I might be more open."

Lola: "I will be your vulva."

Back to the carnivorous waterbed, Aglaia heaves and dips and perches herself like a fortress on top of Ela, breasts first and heaviest, and squashes her so that they can fuck face to face and clit to clit, like fighting bulls.

Oprah's saliva burns Ela's face like astringent.

Suddenly, Aretha changes her mind, gets up, giving Ela some breathing time, plays an overused gravelly record of the "Swanlake" soundtrack, pulls up her imaginary sleeves like Mamabear ready to clean house and, dancing the White Swan pas-de-deux, launches a full-blown attack on Ela's unsheltered body.

Ofra uses her rough feline hard-as-a-shoe-sole tongue, her broken pointy teeth and brutal fingerstubs that are each thicker than an erect cock and do not wither with wear, buries her hot red face between Ela's legs in a gross crass attempt at 69 which is impossible as Ela's mouth can reach just below Isadora's breasts, and sucks hard like a vacuum cleaner.

Squeezed between the whopping bulk of this female gladiator and the wobbly wet mattress, suffocated in pain and pleasure, crammed and cracked and swooning under sexual overkill, as Acapella's immense mouth drills into her still healing vaginal cavity and sucks life from her, Ela realizes:

a. her frame is too small and frail to withstand the coming lust, and this may turn out to be her last fuck;

b. without its previous elasticity, her gaping cavity will experience unspeakable tortures in the hands of this maenad and may even get chopped up again before Ela knows it;

c. this stolid woman will tread in her footsteps forever after if Ela doesn't rush into a quick exit at once, for this unfathomable body will put a claim on her own;

d. Ela's mounting uneasiness is now slasher-genre terror;

e. the waterbed is quickly breaking down under them.

So despite her bliss at being fucked by such a grand female torrent, despite her urge to leave herself in the hands of this behemoth, Ela labours to rise from under Yalta's pressure and to motion to her that the bed is leaking. But as she opens her mouth to shout, she comes from both mouth and womb in profusion.

It is Ela's first full orgasm since her separation from her runaway cunt and her subsequent bereavement. It is such a joy to come, and to know that she can come! She wants to celebrate.

Wondering if this stark two-woman duel represents her new sexual pattern, Ela screams at the top of her lungs in order to let busy Matilda know that she has come and thus she now deserves a moment's rest.

Belinda lifts her big furious face, smiles proudly like a child who has pulled off a prank, notices the thin silver vomit trickling from Ela's mouth and frowns motheringly: "AIDS?"

Ela: "I am sorry, I can't stop coming."

Malta: "A funny thing happened to me as I was coming: I wanted to die for a noble cause."

Ela: "Waterbeds make me seasick." Her post-orgasmic voice resounds sweet and heavy, like a priest's caress.

Ida: "Strong feelings never bother me. Can I go on now? I am enjoying you tremendously; like fucking my own cunt. Redemption does a lot for me."

Ela points to the torn shrinking mattress that is reduced to a wrinkled bluish plastic sheet sunk under a large pool of stalesmelling water and cum, and then shakes her head emphatically.

Splashing about, the two women progress into the standard casual post-sex chat which Ela has initiated. Moving cautiously on her hands and buttocks, Ela struggles to pull herself away from the slippery bed without breaking her bones.

Paola, dripping streams of sweat that add to the wet mess, sits up and lights a Fidel cigar.

Ela: "I politely take my leave."

Luella: "Do you at this instant intuit the absence of God?"

Ela: "Who? You know nothing about me!"

Lucinda: "As I look at your beauty, I want to sit on the curb or crawl into my bed and cry like a child, with snot running down my manly lips. After 28 years in therapy, I have a right to say: I am not unloved. If I let you out of my hold, it is only to get a better view of your short slender thighs, your tiny pale waist and your hard round ass."

Ela, tempting the fates as she is making her escape from inside the wolf's hot wet belly: "You can crush me; you can put me in a crate and mail me to the Near East; crystallize me and drink me in your tea; cremate me and eat me in soups; crinkle me between the pages of your Bible or stretch me out on your roof to dry and then expose me in a fancy neon-lit glass case; you can start a collection. But names will never hurt me."

Helena: "You look like a fast-spreading fire. Some things simply don't die. Be careful with yourself: is it windy out?"

Ela goes home and lights up the fireplace. She listens to Stravinsky's *Firebird*, crouches next to the mirror and hears a growl in her stomach. She thinks: "I am not even a woman who bites her nails." The firelight flares in her big eyes, and they in turn flare in the mirror. She is stunned by the unworldly flowerlike youth that looks back at her, animated with shrill pleasure like a choking girl on a rollercoaster. She suddenly resembles her cunt. A new thought blazes through her mind: "Am I my own lost cunt?" The fire blazes up. Ela wants to jump in it.

Meanwhile, in the same city, her cunt is flooding the world market, oblivious to Ela's complex predicament.

I'M WRITING ABOUT SALLY

MARK LEYNER

Interestingly enough, I starred in "South Pacific" for two years before negotiating oil rights with the Shah of Durani and then performing delicate eleventh-hour dermatological surgery upon Birgit Nilsson at the Gloucester County College Hospital in Sewell, New Jersey, and now I'm writing about Sally.

To 50% of you, that proportion which does not know me—that proportion of you to whom I am a total stranger, "Sally" shall refer to Rachel Horowitz my girl friend in actual life. To the other 49%, those of you who know me on a personal basis, through correspondence, those of you who are even familiar with me solely on the basis of telephone calls ("Hello, Baseline Toyota?" "No, you have the wrong number." "How's Wednesday look for a thousand mile check?" "Wednesday looks crowded. How's Friday for you?" "Super." "Bring a change of clothes.") "Sally" simply represents an obsessive gesture in the metalanguage of "naming," in other words, a kind of distant love—a real doll—a ghost with a winning smile, who I'd like to have visit me over the Columbus Day weekend—that's the weekend of the 8th.

Sonny Liston remodeled my nose in the fifth round in a

Las Vegas ring.

I wrote a monograph on bubbles and then became the proprietor of a ginseng establishment and my best friend is some clam from Cheyenne.

Yesterday, the 13th of September, a conference was summoned to London to settle a new map of the Balkans. It became evident by lunchtime that Austria's prime object was to deny Serbia direct access to the Adriatic. And, of course, behind closed doors, Austrian ministers' jingoism waxed turgid in the grand huff and puff manner. The resolution of Austria to keep Serbia out of Albania was matched by the determination of Russia that the Serbs should be given this access to the sea. It was so silly! By 2:00 P.M. Europe was brought to the brink of war and by 2:30 P.M. war was averted. Like ad hoc big brothers, the Germans exercised a moderating influence over the Austrians, the English over the Russians. Hardly was the ink dry upon the settlement than acrimonious quarrels broke out among the very political "siblings" themselves. The ramshackle state of European stability reminds me of the state of Sally's furniture. The edge of her bedroom dresser is marred. The wicker is broken, and the vinyl worn on her dining-room chairs. The cushions are worn on her couch and plastic tubing in the welting is coming out of the corners. The legs on the dining room table are loose and need regluing.

Sally—

I don't know how to title these times—perhaps "The Contamination of Happiness" or "Bewildered, and Bereft of Funtimes" or maybe "Here Comes Hell Again!"—I miss you so much I want to have fits. There's no news—only a revolving span of drudgery and discontent—barely marked by the passing of the days which speed by with the swiftness of a buried ton. The people I meet might as well be on the moon. I keep thinking, and each time as another realization, what a wonderful superb person you are. I just want to be with you. Maybe this weekend I'll put the pen to a cheerier letter.

All my love,
Mark

The Boston Celtics put me on waivers when I manifested the stigmata of Christ—I couldn't shoot without discomfort. I'm an Irish raconteur and I entered the Story Fest in order to win enough cash to buy Sally some new furniture. As soon as the judge said "Go!" I had to render flies in three different ways:

"I'll teach you the abc's of dance," I said and Sally said, "We gotta get some zzz's" and I began to shimmy unavailed upon, but then, at the western portico, a head popped up and we both saw it, you know what I mean?—and we just knocked that expensive oeil-de-boeuf style window right out in our enthusiasm to intercept the mannerless guy.

"I am zee zinger who zings at Anthony's Abattoir Sur La Mer," he said, bowing crisply—and his back crackled.

"Perfect" I said, "Now we can certainly dance, see—he'll sing and we'll dance.

"Nix" Sally said, "Shall I hit the hay alone or will you join me?"

"Loosen up," I suggested, doing a few quick squats, nipping at her tail at each descent.

"I run tomorrow in The Big Stakes you randy lunk—

lemme sleep."

Needless to say I did everything to keep her up including putting flies on her behind. I didn't go to the event the next day but ascertained via reliable source that she ran like molasses.

The next night after another scene, I vowed to sell her—"I'm through with horses," I adjured. I took a whore's bath, zipped over to the club and in the enthusiasm of my watershed pledge, I split a card in two, sideways, and burst about four thousand seven hundred balls in ten hours of continuous shooting.

I was a bit hard pressed as I approached the second way:

> The guerillas are the fish—
> the people are the sea...

"No, no! " the judge shouted, "You got the fly motif not the fish motif. Get lost and don't come back!"

With the sangfroid of an oyster on Sunday, I accepted the nonetheless unpalatable notion that I had been foiled. I suppose I'm really quite frightened of flies.

I vant to be as mysterious as a voman.

Dear Mao,

I hope the people in heaven are real together. If they're not, I know you're organizing them.

Sincerely,
Kathy

The workers in the old factory were laughing so much!

Someone had just told the funniest joke! "A Yankee goes into a drugstore to buy condoms. 'I'll have a package of rubbers," he says. The druggist takes them from the shelf, 'That'll be $3.50 with tax.' 'I don't want the ones with tacks,' the Yankee says, 'I want the ones that stay up by themselves!'"

> "You know, you look too nice to be in a dump like this. What brought you here?"
>
> "You're a queer one, you're young," she said. "Love brought me here."
>
> She laughed, and the laugh was harsh with the hint of tears behind it. She threw back her head, and touched the rose in her black hair. She had a lot of hair.
>
> —from *Confidential*
> by Donald Henderson Clarke

You see me with my sunglasses and cigar at ringside—then in the morning—it's the 14th of September—I had bought a purple toothbrush to clean my tongue and imagine a voluptuous coed—a pouting libertine in men's pajamas—a girl paring her eyelashes with the scissors my father had used for his nose hairs—a Hoffritz scissors! Some cowboy told me an eastern scissors won't cut at this altitude...who do they take me for? Do they want to see me cry like Jackie Coogan in "Toyota Sally"?

(This section should be read like a Jewish Haggadah.)

I began to think of my employees as students—two of whom were intrigued by the image of a hypertrophic drummer beating upon a bus-like gong. The re-juxtaposition of words, that is, simply, the manipulation of language, from a position within the matrix of a consumer society, (such as U.S.A.), or from within the matrix of a draconian society (such as ours) is an analogous operation to one which I undertook a number of days ago and which I wish to render: I awoke on the morning of the 10th of September and divided my body up into square centimeters and upon each cm. applied a different cologne—in point of illustration, upon one nearly matted area beneath my pitching arm I daubed what is commercially known as "Canon & Common Law"—a fusty bouquet with the slightest hint of sherry and damp tweed; upon the raised demarcated square at the base of what Sean Michaels calls the "milch pimple" I applied the somewhat rousing fragrance of "Turkish Scimitar." At any rate, each of the thousands of square cms. was "bathed"—as it were, in like fashion. The experiment consisted of, procedurally, simply this: entering a full early-morning bus and evaluating the response, particularly the distaff response to, first, the cumulative effect of the odeur and secondly the particular effects of each "flesh-tag", as it was exposed to the air. I was at the time completely unaware of the fact that similar experiments conducted in Quebec City under the aegis of the Canadian Royal Academy had resulted inexplicably in epidemic-style outbreaks of (with each affliction a drop of wine should be poured into the plate) Bugger's Itch, Bilge Mouth, Fad Dieting, Listless Advertising, and infrequently, Ridiculous Judicial Appointments. The bus rocked back and forth like a buoy and before I could collate any substantial data a behemoth percussionist had set his giant mallet upon the top of the bus and its metallic richness resounded throughout Boulder calling all writers to work. Boulder's a writer's town; its streets bespeak the tangled strains of the raconteur's spiel. "Sally" I said to the girl sitting next to me, "Is that my wallet you have? Do you have any relatives with irritating habits? Is an olfactory art plausible?" Just then we careened into the old factory—the place where great literature is made—the place where many of the great classics were written including, most recently, Thelma Strabel's *Reap The Wild Wind* and my own "In Susan."

She insisted upon reading and re-reading "In Susan" and talking technique.

She pointed to my nose. "Run into a hammerfish?" she asked.

The next morning I wrote her a note:

> In response to your question—how well do we know Susan—it seems to me that the question should not be—how well do we know Susan vis-a-vis the notion of character qua character—but how well do we "know" Susan qua Susan—a question which synecdochically raises the corollary—how do we "know" "In Susan" qua "In Susan"—at which point, the word "know" seems to spasm like a fish out of water.
>
> I've recently begun a new tack...now I'm writing about the agent of my twenty-four hour-a-day anxiety. Listen closely...he's like a madman on the loose. His footsteps approach with each creak of the floorboards above. I can hear his bell. He murmurs, "Sally's forgotten you..."

She lay in the sand with her scuba mask, snorkel, spear and flippers and I built, like the bowerbird, a chamber in which to woo her. To woo her hence. To woo her from the gloss of the page. I looked at the clock-radio, at the photograph of Sally upon the night-table and again at the photograph in the magazine. My laziness annoyed me—there were three matters which required my immediate attention: the unraveling of a blunderheaded confusion regarding my bank account, the acquisition of a New York Times and the purchase of Donald Henderson Clarke's newest volume entitled *Confidential*. I was especially anxious to see the size of the headline announcing the Kaiser's break with the Prussian Parliament. I called two of my students and told them to get right over with the new palanquin and take me to the bank, first of all!

I precipitated the disco wave by using a bat bone on a woman's ear as a sort of musical dildo. The song went like this:

I know I've said and done stupid and upsetting things in the past—but please believe me, I want to be with you always—I just want us to be together for good. I have absolutely no interest in any one else—that's simply the fact of it. Uh-huh Uh-huh!

I'm not going to talk about who should move where or stay where or anything like that—I just want to tell you that I hope in the coming weeks we can make some plans (be they present or future plans) to stay together and perhaps get married. Uh-huh Uh-huh!

> I just want to know for sure that our relationship is permanent—because knowing that will make whatever separation there is more than bearable. I'll talk to you soon.

Ah...if only nuptials were Sally's bag. Perhaps she's too much of the whore.

The sheets smell like Sally. There's snow on the mountain already. Is Sally alive? Has she been driven to resort to cannibalism? Has she simply been driven to a resort—perhaps Steamboat Springs?

I attended, uninvited, a soirée in Louella Menzies' smoky trailer. Nothing had yet been served and during a lull I fairly burst out, "Did somebody say dinner was on? What is the conventional wisdom vis-a-vis dinner, because I need the sustenance to make way like a smitten red-man into each valley and canyon where I'll cup my hands to my mouth and call, 'Yoo-hoo...Sally...yooo-hooo!' "

WHEN SLEEP COMES DOWN

ROB HARDIN

To Liz Brockman, whatever she is: alive, dead or dreaming.

When the telephone rang at four am, in a loft cluttered with scores and music notebooks—notebooks seared and starred with expressive markings like seismographs of restrained psychosis—Gizmo hadn't been sleeping. He'd been jerking off slow motion to the voice he heard now: the voice on the receiver, a sample from his wettest nightmare. That drawl in a sandpaper rasp belonged to Jill, the girl he'd been picturing off and on for seventeen hours. He tried to make her say where she was, but she kept changing the details. "In a bar," "with some friends," "on the corner"—whatever the location, the exchange that was probably taking place made his eyes crinkle. She was broke, straight and shivering. To take care of her problem, the mode of commerce was sex for D.

He pulled on his camouflage raincoat and booked. Outside, the rain had just let up, and the sidewalks of Alphabet Town were as slimy as the skin of a queen termite. He checked all the streets in his neighborhood, then the abandoned buildings. He pretended he wasn't looking for her, just to free his peripheral vision. But it was when he'd really given up—not told himself he had—that he found her at last.

He pulled her out of a rusted Plymouth by a fistful of hair so close to the scalp that at first it felt unrecognizable. But the blonde ponytail he'd tugged compulsively for nine months had been abbreviated to match some trick's twist. As he dragged her through the empty windowframe, the first thing he saw was a Tenaxed flat-top dyed auburn. Her face came into the light without a wince of discomfort—her tanned complexion ravaged by skin popping, her eyes one-sided, like limo glass.

But her figure had grown so vivid in his imagination that he didn't have to decipher the darkness in order to replay a slow pan: high breasts, a torso like an hourglass thickened, an ass so full that when he spanked her, it quivered, the brown swell darkening to a deep rose. Even like this—fucked unconscious—she was fine enough to have ridden in a rich trick's Lincoln until he left her there, used and useless.

When she was half-way out of the car, an empty bottle of hycotuss expectorant slid across her chest: prescription codeine. She'd probably raided some college girl's medicine cabinet and spent the night here because she hated the rain as much as she feared her own intelligence.

He spread open her corduroy jacket. Slow motion roaches crawled out of the pocket: a sugar donut fell out, half-eaten. She was feeding the bugs again, as narcotics ate away the fist between her ribs.

She'd written a message on her wrist in red ink: **Princess of Morticians.** That's what she'd called herself on the phone, her English lit mind remembering Thomas Lovell Beddoes as her body leaned against the booth, performing acts. She'd called just to know she had an out, a faraway squeeze in the granite world. Because he was the boyfriend whom junky girls picture when they dream of kicking. (They don't need to clean up—yet—they just want to keep him on file.)

She was a sick twist, which was why he dragged her into a cab and home to his mattress. She was nearly a toss-up, but that didn't matter: he was drawn to her death-trance eyes, to her olive skin, to those cheek-bones so high and chiselled they were like Hepburn in plaster of Paris, a statue poised too close to the window, so that soot and rain had changed the smooth texture into something the blind could read.

As soon as he'd dropped her onto his bed, he pulled off her jeans. She wasn't wearing panties. He touched her pussy and it was wet. He sniffed his fingers, but they didn't smell like semen.

"I'm always tracking you down and you always look worse than you did the night before."

"Huh?...Giz...I feel like...what are you doing..."

They were naked now and he was fucking her awake. "I've been saying your name, Jill. I licked you some, but you were already wet. I thought you could hear me."

"No, but...it's okay...just let me go to the bathroom."

When she staggered back to him, he set her down gently and slid it in. The feeling was even better than he remembered. He fucked her until the haze faded from her eyes, and she was holding onto him like the last girder of sanity's bridge.

"...it hurts, Giz...fuck me harder..."

He imagined he was fucking her in the alley with the rats and the piss-smell and the shattered glass. He imagined dying with her, walking her through the graveyard until she could do it herself, sort of, tromping stiffly down the darkening path in soiled white lace, a firefly crawling up her arm. Until they were all the way into the woods, branch-shadows closing on her singed whiteness, the gray sky massing to black. As if night were crawling over her, a cluster of spiders.

His come was dust in a bone-saw paradise. When he finally looked down, he saw *nothing*. Her body grinned up at him, her bone structure the mirror of a rictus smile.

They lay there for hours, warm and distracted. She didn't make promises because he wasn't in the mood to listen. So when she excused herself to go to the bathroom, he was half-aware. He didn't pay much attention when she took her crumpled coat with her.

When sleep came down, he thought absently about a song he was writing for a new artist, an industrial artist for the alternative department at Atlantic. He lay there trying to be patient long after the inspiration had faded. When he finally knocked on the bathroom door, nearly an hour had passed. She was probably shooting up in there. That was like her—to lean behind bathroom doors, hating herself until the rush came and she hated no one. *I should've checked her pockets for works,* he thought as he opened the door.

Her corpse was keeled over beside the fixture's porcelain base, crumpled on the floor, one arm still braced against her stomach. Her eyes were wide and pinned. Her muscled body was beautiful even in agony, and now it was empty. The emblem of a dead soul.

He carried her outside and dumped her in an abandoned building. He had to, he told himself—it was either that or get nailed for possession. He was in the music business, and he was so known for lacking vices that people called him "The Bishop": "Man, that dude don't do nothin'. He so straight he lookin' to become a minister." With studio clients who pay double-scale by the hour, a drug rep was the wrong kind to have. Sentimentality is a bad substitute for respect.

For days, he walked around stricken, imagining her voice, her tits dangling over him. When he thought of her, he wept, telling himself he loved her. But what he really loved was death. She was marked for it as surely as track marks had burned decay's history into her arm. He himself didn't do drugs. He wanted death's embrace vicariously, to feel the arms close over him while he was fully conscious, fully hard, feeling the come shoot out of him like an arpeggio.

Each night at dusk, at four am, when he remembered her, his purple thoughts acquired a black sheen. Buried by strangers, forgotten by friends, it seemed that her image was being replayed in his mind alone. Recalling her last night on earth made him feel like Dowson inside, an Edwardian drinking himself to death in pain and shame. Or staggering down brick inroads, a mongrel clipped by hooves. Transfixed by the carriage lantern as the nightwood wheeled to blackness.

GUNPOWDER COME

ROB HARDIN

He spotted her on the Fourth of July in a place misted with the smoke of cherry bombs. Krane was standing in the doorway of Embargo Books, listening to "Do It Like A G.O." by the Geto Boys. Rap lyrics and the smell of gunpowder made Norfolk Street feel like a site of terrorist resistance. But slogans of defiance turned alchemical when a figure emerged from the tinted fumes.

She came into view slowly, turning the corner as the yellow haze began to clear. Something was wrong with her face—it was a tragi-comic mask of slackness and rigidity. But beneath this oxymoronic expression lay the cast of a Botticelli angel: Roman nose, flared nostrils, wide, dark eyes like those of a cat in shadow. She was quite beautiful, even though she had been tortured to the point of temporary paralysis.

A bracelet of string dipped in blood and cerebro-spinal fluid had been knotted around her wrist. Intricate with tangles, its drippings were medieval and complex, a lithographed waterfall of crosses and scythes. Had this decoction of tears been drawn from her body or her lover's? Both had been imprisoned under the guise of drug auditing, but only one had emerged to meet him. Was she being released out of mercy, or to warn him of the consequences of rebellion?

As she approached, the temperature of his body changed in sympathy. He touched her fist and shivered when it opened like a torsion of frost. His nerves, a microskein of filaments, accessed her sense-memory, compelling teletacit voices to *shriek* more information about her ordeal than CIA interrogators could hope to extract.

She had been broken into like a box of murder. After twisting her head apart in search of explosives, suppression probes had found only semantic fragments—secrets in a language so evanescent that it passed for air. But Krane knew why she was crypted inside. His nerves reached through the veneer of transparence, probing like antennae for the bloody country behind the wall.

Chained to the corpses of her own family for weeks, she'd learned to associate the proximity of love with the maggots of decomposition. Interrogators had starved her until she was forced to reify the faces of her loved ones—first with revulsion, then with hunger. In the official report, CIA clerks had suggested that her paralysis was the result of a disease caused by cannibalism, but this was unlikely. Precipitated by famine, exhaustion and dehydration, the climax of her stroke was physical collapse.

Scenes of death had become sites of orgasm. Her legs nearly buckled as she tipped her pelvis toward Krane, chilling his synapses with spurts of information. Seconds of pleasure swelled into pictures which obliterated the reality of Norfolk Street: her legless mother, opened at the waist. The castrated cadaver of her father, cheekbones blunted by sandpaper. And at the center of a prison floor, an excrescence of tissue and pliant marrow: the remains of her four-month-old son. The interrogators had opened his screaming smile with knives; it was only at the moment of release that she could endure his rape. Tortured by the absence of torture, her come was dust. A sandpainting of empty bodies and fixed lamprey eyes.

SEX GUERRILLAS

BY HAROLD JAFFE

Tough Tiddy Thursday: Wheat toast and coffee followed by hexagonal blue pill with apple juice. Drive to F and Kissinger, Bell-Tel Marriott over there.

Display tag, get admitted. S/he's waiting in lobby, leaning against a Greek Revival pillar, Corinthian, I think, watching animal cartoons on one of the monitors, cracking her gum.

"You humid?" I say.

"I'm always humid," s/he says.

We skip into the elevator that goes to the "tower," only get out one floor below. Set the magnet on the door channel to keep it from closing. Coordinate digitals, wait eighty-three seconds, remove the magnet, get back into the elevator, stick gum over the tiny camera head, press T, kick out of our clothes.

Elevator stops at tower but door remains closed. Flashing red warning light goes off. We're nekkid.

My name is Dos. S/he's Una.

S/he: "You've got a fresh tattoo."

Me: "You've got some fresh rings."

S/he: "I find a hole, I stick a ring through it. I sure like your tattoo."

Me: "Wanna lick it, wanna taste it?"

S/he sticks out her tongue, pink, moist, and longer than you'd think.

"Ah, oh, yes, YES, oh, WEE-OO."

Good, hot sexing.

"Shoot your jizz," s/he sighs.

Splat, splat, splat...splat, splat...splat...splat, splat...

Just about all the floor buttons greasy with jizz. I missed # 23, but that's showbiz.

Get dressed, coordinate digitals, remove gum from camera head, press L for lobby. Elevator moves. At the lobby, Bell-Tel security bozos shoot puzzled, angry stares at us. But what can they do, right?

⁂

Furry Fisted Friday: Halfbowl of granola, coffee, hexagonal blue pill. Check under the hood. Get in, burn rubber, catch graffiti freeway south.

Una waiting at the ramp, near the pink oleanders, I can see "her" quarter of a mile away, legs folded under chin, cracking her gum, staring at the tiny TV monitor.

Pull onto the shoulder and s/he slides next to me, touch tongues.

I exit right, re-enter north, graffiti highway, like I said. Acrobatic twelve-year-old guerrillas with spray cans and retractable ladders have done a number on the freeway. Anagrams, ideograms, logos, gang communicadoes, coded shit. One gang sprays on a stanchion, competing gang sprays on a billboard. Media compare them to animals scenting territory. Well, what do you think art is? Plus, they do their shit before dawn, so who's gonna ketch 'em?

We're heading north to Orange, Disney, that deal.

Una has the CD on real loud, Madonna before they offed her.

"You get to sleep last night?" s/he says.

"Not really. You?"

"Not really."

Traffic building. I'm swerving in and out of lanes. At Zoo Drive, south of Oceanside, I climb onto the median between north and south and Tres pops out, scoots into the front seat. Tres hands Una a pink oleander, me a white one.

Did I say my name is Dos?

Scamper back onto the freeway.

"They're poison—oleanders," Una says.

"So's the air we breathe," Tres says.

"So's the water we drink," I pipe in.

"So's the food we eat," Tres says.

"So's the puss we lick," from me.

"Dick too," from Tres. "Asshole too."

"I don't believe it," Una says. "How can sweet sex be poison?"

Una's slipped another CD in—Public Enemy before they went MTV.

Tres is slipping out of "his" clothes.

4:20: brake lights and congestion in Orange County.

4:35: bumper to bumper.

Una and Tres, naked in the backseat, are doin' some shit.

Other cars see, point, honk their horns.

Una climbs into the front seat, takes the wheel. I'm naked in the back with Tres, doin' some shit.

Traffic stops dead just south of Anaheim, near the Disneyland exit. Which means Una, Dos, Tres in the backseat doin' some shit: pull-push-slide-slick-lick-bite-slither-spray jizz through the back window, get some on the jacked-up, oversized tires of a GMC longbed pickup. Driver, bare-chested, tattooed dude with his cap turned back to front, can of Coors in his fist, grins like a fool, flashes us thumbs-up.

✣

Sag Ass Saturday: Wheat toast, coffee, hexagonal blue pill.

Pick up Tres and Quatro. Una has the day off, visiting her grandma in Needles, she's real old.

We drive northwest to one of the biotech complexes. There's a clot of them. Genetic engineering, in vitro micro-manipulation, animal experimentation. Plus it's business as usual on Saturdays.

Great spot, this one, on the ocean. Hell, lab techs wouldn't know ocean if it squirted up their colon.

Anyway we park by the ocean and double back. On the northwest side is a double roof, receding superstructure. Boost ourselves up on the lower roof, make our way to the large bay window which looks out to the sea, into the dining hall where techs in their white lab frocks flecked with test-animal blood dine. It's 12:35, the large space is full.

We're in workclothes, carrying implements: shovel, metal pail, paint rollers. The techs notice us as they eat their institutional quiche or stew or tofu while gazing at the ocean. They look surprised when we lay down our implements, undress, lube each other, commence to tug, suck and fuck. Have you ever seen a biotechnician express surprise? Well, the whole nerdy dining room is watching us in astonishment, some with fork or spoon poised between plate and agape jaws.

The large bay window is noise-proof, but we can tell that

no one utters a word. Faint sounds of cutlery, a stray cough, thick breathing.

We paint their window to the ocean with jizz.

✣

Semiotic Sunday: Hexagonal blue pill and juice. No food. Fasting and church on TV. Prayer-packs.

✣

Mambo Hipped Monday: Oatmeal, coffee, hexagonal blue pill.

Una, Dos, Tres, Quatro, Cinco, Seis. We're off to the bank. Which one? Wells Fargo. Stagecoach, branding iron, chaps, Indian kills, Duke Wayne, roll-yr-own.

It's noontime, long queues.

Six of us in line, one behind the other, we swap spit, feel each other up a little. Through the clothes.

Draw some nasty looks, sure, but nobody says anything. We know we're on camera, but who ain't?

So we ratchet up a notch, probing hands and fingers under clothes, sucky kisses, earlickings.

Well, the bank guard comes on over, tells us cut it out.

We do, but then start it again, the six of us, changing partners, dryhumping, sighing, but one behind the other, maintaining the order of the line.

Guard comes over again, threatens to throw us out. Except we wave our checks and money at him.

Quatro says: "Where in the bank's bylaws does it say anything about sexual conduct while in line?"

Bank guard glares at Quatro.

"You ain't so bad," Cinco says to the guard. "Take out your

gun, I'll stick a yellow flower in it."

Guard retreats, glowering.

We start up again. Meanwhile the line is moving and Una is at a window transacting money business. Cinco has tenderly unzipped Tres's organ. Everyone could see it. One of the customers in line actually shouts (which is something you rarely hear in a bank): "Put that organ back in your pants."

Instead, the rest of us display *our* organs.

The guard is back with his hand on his holstered Colt.

"This is a b-b-bank," he sputters.

Tres says: "Why don't you leave the Colt in the holster and show us your organ."

Another guard—two more—appear, strong-arm us out of the bank.

"You come in here again, we'll jail your ass," younger guard shouts at us outside.

Una, who has finished "her" bank window transaction, comes out at that minute and says: "You can jail us but you'll never jail our asses."

✣

Tuesday Dues Day: Like a rash after eating strawberries, it's another urban uprising, called "riot." Broke out suddenly and is radiating out of the inner city ghettoes.

I said it was a rash, but it's also a tidal wave, tornado, tsunami, earthquake. Has nothing to do with the shit we've been made to swallow from day one, right?

What you have then are enraged folks fucking despite the edicts.

TV claims we're black and brown males, gangbangers,

child abusers, drug abusers, but that's a lie. We're females, males, in-betweens, all colors. Moist and soft and hard, sweet-smelling. It's as though someone spiked the water supply with X. Ecstasy to you. The mind police are beside themselves. Cuz we're doing it in the streets, on the roofs, in convenience stores, in municipal offices. *In the banks*! Problem is TV can't report it "live" because everyone and their mom is nekkid.

✣

Witch Hunt Wednesday: Wheat toast, coffee, hexagonal blue pill.

Was just about to turn off the TV when they kicked the door open, burst in, Uzis, Sig Sauers, clubs, big shined-up shoes. Spread my legs against the wall, hit me hard in the groin, thighs, dragged me out, tossed me in the paddy. Una, Tres and Quatro in there too. Didn't let us talk.

Not jail like we expected but a football stadium is where they took us. Couple thousand of us it looked like standing there on the astroturf. Shitload of TV cameras.

I don't know who gave the signal, or whether anybody actually did, but we all kicked off our clothes and started touching and playing with each other. But then the guards got into it, clubbing us, kicking.

That night, late, they made us strip and lined us up on the astroturf, two abreast. Then they marched us, twenty or thirty at a time, into the lockers—what used to be the lockers—under the stadium.

Someone cried out: "Can you smell it? It's gas."

Ebony Man

RICARDO CORTEZ CRUZ

Beats & Pieces/No Connection/Smoke Dis One/People Hold On/Fat (Party And Bullshit)

—Coldcut *from the album,* What's That Noise?

Ebony man had a hatchet face but it was no excuse for him to have hung around Rooster in the ghetto-starving, in the evil mix of the city, in the slum-life, in Compton, in hiding, in Hell because just like that it could take your breath away.

Rooster, his homie, was never Buddy Love. On several occasions, Rooster worked ebony man's nerves by calling him Chops and talking smack that ebony man had a fat, ugly face hewn out of a chocolate block by a hatchet. Rooster was a bitch who took everyone's leavings and turned them into fresh eggs. So it came as no surprise when the LAPD found him dead on some Black woman's porch, blood all over his penis and drawers, dirt and shit in his mouth. Rooster had lived large til then. When he was waxed, some m.f. in the local neighborhood asked the question what came first, "Rooster or the eggs and shit," since Rooster was a fucking machine. He and ebony man were sweet on one another until Rooster quit it. When Rooster was iced, ebony man bought a one-way ticket to St. Louie and broke town, nausea in his stomach, his big head in the clouds tripping about the American way and only a bag of peanuts to eat. Ebony man never knew any of Rooster's other friends but was glad he didn't. It wasn't easy being a fat man on the move. Sometimes being fat left Chops breathless, without life insurance. He would have been gone forever if it were not for the fact that he forgot to tell Kalier "see ya'" and quit his DJ service where he played oldies-but-goodies and take-me-back tunes for his old lady and girls who walked backward in a high wind. The news of him leaving Compton would probably fuck up Kalier's life, but Chops would give it to her gently.

He would do almost anything for her, except take abuse. He didn't like to take abuse. Once, his old lady called his fat the density that ended his shape. Chops/ebony man paid Rooster fifteen fucking dollars to fuck her but later decided against it. Rooster almost did her anyway but ebony man paid him off to stop.

"Money is the root of evil," Rooster said, "but the lack of it is almost as bad."

Those words came back to haunt Chops, bit by bit. But when the fat lady sang at Rooster's funeral, ebony man thought "the thang" was over. For once in his life, he felt like dancing.

Stupid-fresh in the memory of Rooster, ebony man, once guilty of hiring a hatchet man to do his girl, did the fandango with a hatchet inside his right sock—his tuxedo clinging on, face black, back arched, bent fingers pulling on the frayed dreadlocks of gray carpet, toes like piano keys. He stood and watched his feet. His toes moved wildly as if they were being played by Jerry Lee Lewis.

He cut the rug.

John Coltrane blew out his jaws, blood all over the sax.

But, ebony man kept dancing. He did the rumba.

The neighbors knocked on the floor. "What the heck you doing up there?" they shouted. They sounded like peeping Toms.

He ignored them, their knocks like tic-tocs counting the time before he would put a hole in his head.

Oh, his head. His head was black with a X to mark the spot. His head was the *Boston Globe* crying about AIDS and muggings. The headaches would take him out if the drugs (Arm etc.) didn't.

His head started talking to him like a motion picture.

"What, you on the pipe or what?" (Dougie from *Def By Temptation*)

"Not me, baby" (Pookie from *New Jack City*)

"Then shut the fuck up" (Lenny on *I'm Gonna Git You, Sucka'*)

"I'm a closet lover, baby" (Larry Love, *Straight Out Of Brooklyn* by Matty Rich)

Out of it, Chops begged to see Kalier, gold medallions with the word "Peace" around his neck.

"Karen, you know me. I'm Larry Love. Superlover undercover" (Rich)

Straight-up sampling by Chops. Random House. Chophouse. Movies as food for thought.

With his apartment stereo on, Chops did the attitude, a big city concept he saw on Oprah.

The walls shook and a picture dropped downstairs.

"I hate fat people," said Joe, looking at the painting by his feet. He put a bomb in his mouth and lit it.

Upstairs, ebony man or Chops could smell the cigarette burning off time before it put an end to his black ass.

As a tribute, ebony man did the butt, his booty bumping up against the stove in the kitchen, Salt N' Pepa singing "Let's Talk About Sex" on Scotch tape.

Making love on Scotch tape was fucking correctly in his opinion. He could see Kalier with a wheel of tape and a bottle of the good stuff asking him "do ya' feel lucky punk?—well, do ya'?"

He had to move some more. He did the running man, a funky dance he picked up from the Hammer, who grew up in nearby Oakland, California.

He escaped out of the kitchen and dashed into a closet, where he ran into a hanged shirt. He looked up to see what had hit him. The white shirt slipped off the hanger, fell on his fat face and covered his whole head, bagging him like a Klu Klux Klan flour sack. The neighbors shouted, calling him names like "Doughboy," "Ice Cube" and "Mr. Buffalo Butt," while he stood in the closet. He crossed his fingers for luck and felt for the entrance.

Finally, he stumbled out and found himself back in the living room, wondering if he had any Benadryl or Benzocaine or Cortaid or cocoa butter or cost-cutter margarine to put on his fingers for relief.

He rocked back-and-forth on the wood pieces underneath the carpet. The floor gave up: "Move yo' fat ass!" screamed the floor. Some of its ribs were broken.

The natives were getting restless so they knocked harder.

"Hello...hello up there."

"How could you do this to me?" the floor asked.

"Shut up!" Chops yelled. He was no longer going to be dark n' lovely.

He had a slew of magazines on the coffee table in the living room. As he waltzed past the table, he bumped it with his leg and nearly slit his skin on the razor blade he had wrapped around his kneecap. He whirled around and cursed.

He had to calm down. He picked up a copy of *Spin* magazine and flipped through the pictures, slapping them against one another.

He grabbed *Cosmopolitan* and did the same. He made women in the pictures look fat and wrinkled, the way he wanted.

The Pointer Sisters asked, "What have I done to make you feel like dis?"

He shrugged his shoulders, then looked all ugly up against the wall. Having a room of his own wasn't all it was cracked up to be. He was living large in a slaughterhouse, the corner of his living room darkened by the presence of bad granny apples.

For Chops, life was a hospital in which every patient was possessed by the desire to change his bed. It was time for him to kick it.

He leaned back against the dingy wall like a cowpoke with insulation in one hand, dingo boots kicking the wall, spurs spinning and clicking and a keyboard playing a crescendo in his other hand, his eyes cut in his forehead like the slit of an army tank. He dropped the ballistics and spat at the same time Joe threw the butt of his bomb to the ground. Everybody got quiet quick.

Ebony man picked up a fistful of dollars and tossed the money into the air. He waited. Nothing happened. He grabbed a handful of black sequins and threw it up like dust. He waited. Nothing happened. He was real cool about it. His coffee table was a pool table with a broken leg. He grabbed a cue stick, blew chalk dust on the cover of *Cosmopolitan* and shot the eight ball.

He got immediate results: A woman hollered so bad that she almost lost her soul, the stench of chitlins creeping up the stairway toward ebony man's door.

"Annie, are you okay?" asked Michael Jackson, standing in shadows of the hall.

Joe helped her up, dirt on the side of her face.

"Annie, you've been hit by, you've been struck by, a smooth criminal," said Michael.

Meantime, ebony man focused on the nine ball on the table. He went through balls 1-8 like they were nothing. Nine was the last soul remaining. It sat on the corner like a pimp and dared him to shoot.

"Go ahead, punk," it said. "Make my day."

Ebony man leaned his hip up against the table and rocked it, shaking the solids and stripes while they hid under his belly weeping like fat tissue.

Guitarist Jimi Hendrix played "America" as if he had an afro- or ice-pick or something between his teeth.

Then, Ray Charles sung it. Charles' song tingled dude's skin like acid inside a Pepsi cool can.

Following that, Marvin Gaye started singing the "Star-Spangled Banner" live, but the 90-minute tape that was playing reached its end and stopped, killing him.

Ebony man saw himself running down through the cinders of an alley like a chicken, his bare legs hot and peppered with ashes. The night was black as a funeral; a tuxedo covered the moon. And Billy. Billy was chasing his dark ass, coming closer, ready to beat him. "Shoot for the moon, and nothing will stop you," his daddy used to say, even though every year dozens of people have been hurt or killed by falling bullets. Anyway, ebony man flew past a couple of stray cats and sprinted toward the general direction of the moon. He was in trouble. He was hanging on to the tails of night by a single thread. He had a couple of Throwing stars in his pants pocket. He turned around and threw them. Billy was history.

He snatched the billiard ball off the table with one hand and tried to crush it. But when he couldn't squeeze the ball into powder, he tossed it back onto the table, making it squaredance on the surface. The nine ball rolled around the rail cushion before smacking the face of the white ball, knocking it silly with the contact and sending it peacefully into the hole.

Ebony man leaned back up against the dirty wall with the pool stick, plucked a small red apple from his pocket and ate it. His teeth shimmied, chewing on pieces of skin.

He was starting to go crazy. He talked aloud to himself while pondering over what he should do with life.

Downstairs, Joe unwrapped a Band-Aid and stuck it on Annie's forehead. Annie looked up like she couldn't stand the pain.

The floor cracked on ebony man: "You got black feet," it said.

"Shut up!" he snapped. Then, he looked down at his feet to check out the situation. Sure enough, his shit was filthy.

He cracked up.

He was reminded of a joke his daddy told him: "Your apartment is so dirty, it could be a greenhouse."

Ebony man shelved himself along the wall, gazed around at all the magazines and heard laughter.

"Shut up," he said.

His headache was growing worse, like a swollen big toe with no Epsom salts.

Ebony man rubbed his temples and slumped to the floor.

He heard giggling.

"You smell like you got holes in yo' underwear," the floor said. "Get up!"

Ebony man was half-dossing in blue funk; he was both sleepy and tired. He propped his big head up against the cheap paint on the wall and thought about why he had been dancing so much in the first place; flakes were falling off and landing in his hair.

He saw himself going off into The Cotton Club, walking underneath one of those lights that make you look like you a flake. Anyway, ebony man thought about his old lady. The nightclub was where he first met Kalier. Strangely enough, even then she was a steaker.

She was perched on a stool like little Miss-Tuffet when he did the new-and-improved two snaps and a circle, tiptoed up from behind and asked her fine self to dance.

He heard giggles coming from soft, chocolate chip faces that looked closed up inside a cabinet.

"Nerd," she whispered, her long triangular-shaped metal earrings hanging like daggers, dangling like wind chimes against her blushed cheek. The pieces of metal played music together in the breeze of boogie-ing bodies while he stood frozen in the Medieval.

He swore that he saw small frogs and toads and insects and snakes which leapt out of her mouth slinging blood around, landed in his eyes and did his face up like a horror movie.

He fell wounded like Lancelot.

Fresh from *A Rage In Harlem*, she wasted little time in finishing him.

"Pop go da weasel," she said in a New York city accent. Then she chopped him to pieces.

"Well-done, don't you think?" she asked the other women.

As she spoke, her tongue came out like a blade with blood on it.

She sat like a cup at the edge of the round table while men peeped her, hyped her concept and swarmed around her. She loved every minute of it, lashing out with the sharpness of her tongue to catch them.

Hurt, he whipped out a cherry bomb and waved it with his left hand, showing it to the crowd.

There were screams.

"He's got a yonic symbol!" somebody shouted. Then, the crowd began to panic.

"You're a bad man," somebody shouted.

"You ought to be ashamed of yourself," said someone.

"Drop it!" said someone else.

"Take it from him!" said someone.

"Girl, you must be crazy," said someone else.

"Who you talking to, honey?" asked someone.

"Your momma's in the house," lied someone else.

"What's a yonic symbol?" somebody else asked.

"A cherry bomb," said someone.

"As long as it's burning, I don't care," said someone else.

"Please don't hurt, nigger," said a couple of men.

"Who are they?" asked someone.

"That's Joe Blow and his sexually-consenting partners," said somebody.

"He sounds like Bigger Thomas," said somebody else.

"He looks like Clarence Thomas," said someone.

"He probably kisses like Isiah Thomas and Magic," said someone else.

"A peck on the side of the face will get you nowhere in Compton," said somebody.

"Why are they so afraid?" asked somebody else.

"Why are they white?" asked someone.

"Because they're gettin' into our Kool-aid and don't even know the flavor," said someone else.

"Check this out."

"Their faces are pale," said someone.

"White powder around the edges of their nostrils," said someone else.

"White lines in contempt of blood," said someone.

"Pure and simple, they're caining," said someone else. "They inhabit the white spaces." (Someone took out a knife.)

The white boys backed up. "We're dope," Joe said, "because we were born and raised in Compton. Now the motherfuckin' saga continues."

"Cut his lips off if you can find them," said somebody.

"Let's see what he's made of," somebody else added.

The Blacks put the pointed part of the nigger flicker in Joe's mouth. "Pop go da weasel," said someone. It was like he was a rage in Harlem.

Joe starting squirming to break free. A hand came out of nowhere and gently touched Joe on the shoulder.

"Keep hope alive," said a voice.

"Who are you?" asked someone else.

"I am somebody," replied the voice.

The Blacks paused and looked at one another. "Jesse Jackson?" they asked.

"A nigger!" screamed Joe.

"Somebody kill that white boy!" yelled someone.

Ebony man whipped out a match and set the wick of his cherry bomb on fire. The crowd started screaming.

"It's burning!" they shouted. "Run for your goddamn lives!"

"Don't do it," said someone.

"Don't screw with your life," said someone else.

"You gonna' get yourself killed," said somebody else. "Don't do it, son."

But, ebony man would not listen. After first fingering the cherry, dude flicked it up into the air like a great ball of fire.

"Ah-h!" screamed the crowd. It sounded so fake. Then, they ducked under the tables like stunt men in a Hollywood movie. The bomb belly-danced on the floor and then exploded: "Gwa-lah!" it said. Then a trail of thin smoke spelled out "weak."

"Oh shit," said ebony man.

"He didn't have nothing but a kid's firecracker!" screamed the crowd.

"Next time get you a rocket, boy," said the owner.

Ebony man was embarrassed. How he could have brought in a dud was beyond his comprehension. He dashed out the door, hopped on his motorcycle and quickly drove off, his big head waving goodbye in the air as the breeze hit him in the face like popcorn.

Meanwhile, back inside The Cotton Club: "He was kind of cute, wasn't he?" Kalier asked. There was blush on her face which she kept trying to wipe away.

Meantime, ebony man was wiping his eyes in the wind, tasting tears like lemon drops, which went down his throat like hail.

✣

The next day, he woke up with a headache. He walked outside with a martini in his hands and hailshot in his pockets. The trees were bending down as if handing him a peck of apples. He swatted at their branches. "A peck will get you nowhere in Compton," he said. "Step off."

One of the trees threw an apple at his big head. "Here's one for your momma," it said.

Ebony man ran, applesauce in his hair and coming down the side of his face. His big head was spinning, and he didn't know where he was going.

"I must be in Kansas," he thought, "but one bad apple don't spoil a whole bunch of girls."

Somebody drove by from the freeway and called ebony man "nigger," throwing Pebbles at his face.

"Headhunters!" Ebony man concluded. After all, who else would hurl collectibles of used vinyl Soul music towards his neck?

Pebbles was fine, but she couldn't sing worth a damn.

He threw the record down and stepped on it, crushing it but, in the process, slicing his heel as well.

"Hell!" he cried out. Then he flew. As if someone had blew dust in his face, he dashed into the parameters of a black alley, where he dropped dead by the grey garbage cans.

Meanwhile, back at The Cotton Club: Maxi Priest was singing "I just wanna be close to you."

✣

The next day, he woke up and staggered home. Once there, ebony man squirted himself with Mennen and doused his face with Boss. He changed into his blue shirt and black patent leather loafers. He massaged his lizards with mink oil. Then he shot through the wooden door and headed down Tamburine Street, singing "the bitch betta' have my money," the new cut rapped by artists Naughty By Nature.

With The Cotton Club in mind, ebony man two-stepped

his way down the graffiti sidewalks of Tamburine before stopping in his tracks to listen for music. From a distance, he could hear 2 Live Crew saying "Pop That Goochie." He stormed into The Cotton Club and found Kalier rolling on lipstick and lip gloss while talking, party people in the house pointing at her.

"Your show," said ebony man. He approached her like a shadow under a woman's eye.

"Hello," he said. "Would you like to get down?"

She smiled, as all steakers do. She saw the razor stubble on his chin and recognized the Tom Selleck-look. She recognized that he had changed. There was something different about him.

"No, thank you," she answered. Then she reached for a bottle of eyeliner out of her handbag and, with a pencil, stroked it on like India ink.

"I really don't use that much mascara," she said.

"Why use any at all?" he asked. "Back to the dance. You going to shake that booty or what?"

"Not right now," she said. "I don't like this song."

Ebony man didn't want to go. He didn't want to go back with nothing after everyone had seen him ask her to dance. Somebody stopped the music. Ebony man flipped out.

"Damn and shit, did you hear that?" the disc jockey asked. "Homeboy just got turned down twice! Homeboy, you'd better dial 1-800-JESSICA and talk to Jessica Hahn. She'll give you some pub. We'll take up a collection, like they do in church, so you can call her. And, yo, lotti-dotti, why you wanna be so mean to homeboy?"

"I'm not trying to be mean or anything—you can come back and ask me again if they play a better song like Whistle, 'Always & Forever.'"

Ebony man sat down beside her. She knew that he would.

"Has anybody seen my blush?" she asked her girlfriends. They looked clueless.

With his hands fidgeting around with loose change in his pockets, he dropped the dime on her. She knew that he would. He pinched her nipple trying to pick it off her chest.

"Get off me!" she shouted.

He started talking smack at random. She knew he'd do that, too.

"Have you ever heard of the group Fine Young Cannibals?" he asked.

"What?—No more sing-song," she said.

"Let's just kiss and say goodbye," he said. He smiled. She giggled. He laughed. Then they laughed together while she reached for a can of mace inside her purse.

"Why did you come back tonight?" she asked. His face got square. He knew that she knew that he knew she would ask that question.

"You," he said. "Baby, you send me."

A man eavesdropping with a glass of Old Tom in his hands came over and put his hand on ebony man's shoulder.

"Excuse me, sir," said the man. "I'm from Harlequin Books—our motto, 'we love our customers to death'—and I couldn't help but notice that you've got great material there for an incredible nigger romance. If you would just sign here at the dotted line, underneath the small print, you and your yellow Venetian honey over there will be well your way to fame and fortune, the kind they put in magazines, *Ebony* or *Jet*."

"Get out of here!" ebony man said. The Harlequin representative quickly vanished.

"Anyway, forget about me," she said. "You don't even

know me."

"Everything is clear to me," said ebony man. "What else I need to know?"

She rubbed her lips. "You need to know why women are silent," she said. "You need to know why Heaven refuses to give light and the stars refuse to shine. You need to know that it takes two to make a thang go right, and that a woman is something that pays ten cents for a cup of coffee to sit at a lunch counter and blow smoke in men's faces. This and more you need to know."

"Maybe it's obvious I don't understand women," said ebony man. "They'll pay 25 dollars for a slip and be annoyed when it shows and pay five dollars for a bra and dress up for a nightclub by letting it show. A woman's movie is one where the wife commits adultery throughout the picture and at the end, her husband begs for forgiveness."

"So shoot me," she said. "It's clear you magnify your troubles by looking at them through the bottom of a glass. The last time I saw you, you worked your way down from bottoms up. You approached me like an emotional midget who had to climb into a bottle in order to feel like a giant."

"I was having problems."

"Yes, but you could have acted like you had some sense instead of lighting that children's smoke bomb which died on you like a cigarette stamped in an ashtray."

"Yes, but I wouldn't have lit it in the first place if they hadn't pushed me, and if I hadn't been having such a time of it," he said. "But now, my head is starting to clear and I've got big dreams. And, I know I can make it."

"...With a Bloody Mary in your hands," she said. "You left here the other night in such a violent and drunken condition that you failed to realize there were severe storm warnings going on outside. You thought the sirens was the ringing of bells in your ears, so you walked out of The Cotton Club like a big, fat pimp and lost yourself in the middle of the storm."

"Slim, this has happened to me several times," he continued, "but I keep coming back because God has blessed me with nine lives, which surely He would not have done if we were not meant to be together."

"...Which explains the reason He put you in the dumps in the first place, right?" she asked.

"You've got to bottom out before you can get better," he said.

"True, but I've got problems too," she said. "For me, sex is the scream of life that has resulted in a sleepless struggle. I'm addicted. I've got to find a pusher." She got up and rushed to the bathroom.

Ebony man turned and caught a passing waiter. "She's a stripteaser, a skin diva," he said.

The women's bathroom was live. Mints cooled out on the counter. Fresh water fell lackadaisically into the sink and, as a result, was immediately gobbled up. The toilets were clean. And, the toilet paper was scented with Charlie. A woman stood handing out paper towels by the door.

Kalier dove inside the restroom with red-colored lipstick smeared over her hands and the bags under her eyes streaked with black marking. She raced past the attendant and darted to the back entrance of the bathroom.

"I like your skirt outfit," said the attendant. "Turn around, girl, and let me see how it fits in the front."

Kalier popped the door open and threw her arms into the mist. A van filled with cosmetics quickly pulled up to the back door. The driver got out—eating a candy bar—and took a hard-bound book and laid it on top of his hair, mashing it down on his flattop. A homeless brother strolled by, and the driver flipped him the rest of his candy bar, a Whatchamacallit.

"Gee—thanks, man," said the brother. He bit into it before disappearing.

"Johnny, where the hell have you been?" Kalier asked.

"Hey, get off my back!" shouted Johnny. "Everybody's ridin' my jock. Johnny this. Johnny that. Johnny got a gun. Johnny can't read. Johnny's a bad apple. Baby, you must think this stuff comes easy."

"Shut up, Johnny, and give it to me!"

"Don't worry, baby. I'm yo' pusher. I'll take care of you. I'll give you every thang you want."

"Give me two grams of foundation, five tubes of lipstick—various shades, a sealed bag of blush, two bottles of eye-liner, a couple grams of white powder for free-basing and an extra-amount of rouge. Now!"

"What's the rush?" Johnny asked.

"I'm melting," she said.

"I bet you taste like a M & M without the peanut," said the attendant, licking the resin off her lips. "You can melt in my mouth anytime, girl."

"Who are you?" asked Johnny, thinking pussy first.

"Charlie, the attendant."

"Nevermind her—give me the stuff!" Kalier hollered.

Johnny had second thoughts. "I don't know, Kalier. You've had enough. I don't know if we should do this anymore."

"Damn," said the attendant. "It's pretty bad when your pusher won't give it to you. Why don't you just go on home, honey?"

Kalier broke out crying and ran away.

Meantime, ebony man was counting his quarters when

that white man from Harlequin came back with the police.

"There he is!" shouted the man. "He's the one who pulled out his penis, dragged it along the table and showed it to the crowd. I think his name is Jack or something like that."

"I hate a bragging nigger," said one of the officers. "Get him! We'll teach that nigger a thing or two!"

Ebony man grabbed the quarters and his dirty laundry and moved the crowd, flying out into the street where people watched him run.

"Leave me alone!" he shouted back to the police. "You don't know what you're doin'."

The policeman grabbed their Billy clubs. "It's gonna be a long night for you, nigger," they shouted. But, ebony man escaped through the alley.

When he got home, he popped another 90-minute cassette tape into his stereo so he could listen to NWA's "Fuck The Police."

At about 3 o'clock in the morning, he flipped over his tape to change sides and then decided to pack his bags. He grabbed his brush and his Obsession cologne and his blue shirts and threw them into the suitcase. He threw everything into the suitcase.

Suddenly, he heard a knock at the door. He walked casually to the door and opened it, the smell of cigarette smoke clearly strong in the hallway.

When the door was wide open, a raisin-faced woman stood leaning against the rust hinges.

"If you make one more sound, my man says he's gonna bust you in the mouth!" the woman said. Then she turned and walked away.

Ebony man closed the door and heard the lock click behind him. Almost immediately, there was another knock.

He opened the door again and got smacked in the mouth. "Fuck you, fat boy," said some man just before walking away.

Ebony man spat his tooth out and closed the door. There was another knock.

"Who is it?" he asked.

"Open up," the voice said.

Ebony man popped the door and saw Kalier rubbing the make-up off her face, tulips for a mouth.

Kalier saw that ebony man was now wearing polka dots.

"Well, don't just stand there like Fats Domino," she said. "Move out of the way and let me in."

Ebony man did an aside [suck my dick, bitch] and Kalier marched in.

"You're living with me," she insisted.

He cracked up. "Let's go," he said.

She left the room first. He grabbed a meat cleaver, put it behind his back and followed her down the stairway.

"Damn," she said. "It sure is hot in here. I can barely breathe."

Ebony man bit out of a red apple and smiled, looking in silence at her booty, his horns showing.

ON THE UNSPEAKABLE

SAMUEL R. DELANY

the positioning of desire which always draws us to "The Unspeakable" in the first place.

It is an area, a topic, a trope impossible to speak of outside (it is at once evil and extralinguistic) that range, equally difficult to describe, to define: "The Everyday." (*It* is at once banal and representationally difficult.) Both are terribly localized. Both are wholly and socially bounded. The division between everyday and unspeakable, difficult and extralinguistic, banal and evil may just be the prototype for all social division.

We need something from

suck it clean. After three minutes, his hips began to lift in little twitches. He had both hands on his cock now. He shot in a couple or three four-inch spurts that fell, shiny as snot from a November sneeze, down the knuckles of both hands. He raised one and thrust the backs of three fingers into his mouth, turned them over, and sucked away the cum. Then he lifted the other, to lick more off, this time delicately. His tongue reached out pointed, but became broader, slugging slowly between one and the next knuckle, bright with saliva and semen in the

the everyday, then, of a 45-year-old black, gay male who cruises the commercial porn theaters along Eighth Avenue above 43rd Street in New York City (the "Author") in the middle and late 1980s: why not this?

Rose is a pudgy, white, working class prostitute, maybe twenty-six, from Upstate New York; she's also a cracker—which means that for the last few months she's seldom gone for more than ten dollars a trick, since her interests have dwindled pretty much to the next bottle of rocks—a hyperbole if there ever was one: the "bottle," a plastic capsule a shy centimeter long, stoppered at one end with something like they put in the top of Bic pens; the "rocks," about half a crystal of rock salt's worth of cooked-down coke broken up into smaller bits. Cost per bottle anywhere from six to ten dollars. Eight is average. The long-time professional video's flicker he still stared at.

That's when old P.R. beside him woke up long enough to give him a frown.

The white kid jumped a little, rearing to the side, in a hyperbolic moment of fear. (Hyperbole is the figure of the everyday; euphemism is the figure of the unspeakable.) But he gave the guy a look that said, "Say something to me, motherfucker, and I'll bust you!" There was a wholly macho aspect to his exhibitionism.

The old guy shook his head, leaned back against the wall, and closed his eyes again.

The kid went back to licking, moved to the inside of his wrist. With the edge of one thumb he squeegeed up some clam of cum that had fallen on his denim thigh, ate that, and examined his lap and green workshirt for any he'd missed. With a few more tugs he milked his cock of its final freight; then, with hookers working the winter Strip outside have lost all patience with the new breed of "ten dollar whore" crack has created—many of them only fifteen, sixteen, and seventeen years old.

(The meaning of the following exterior urban portrait is entirely in terms of what it tells us of this momentary travesty of theatrical interiority.)

The last three years have seen a radical atmosphere and economic shift along the Strip from the fallout of the cocaine trade—crack, base, eightballs. It's part of the slowly gathering devastation of the entire neighborhood, which is presumably preparing the way for the brave new rebuilding as a large shopping mall, with a few theaters and business towers, scheduled to begin next year: grocery stores, comic-book stores, shoe repair shops, drugstores, barbershops, bookstores, theatrical lighting and make- the hugely circular tongue maneuver five-year-olds reserve for dripping cones, he lapped the last from his fist.

(The above, observed purely as information—his actions and his dress and his bearing, from politeness to belligerence—tell only of what is exterior to this tightly conventionalized and wholly contained commercial, public space.)

Watching him, I found it easy to see the entire nonwhite audience around him—macho, male, a scattering of prostitutes, of transsexuals, of faggots, and largely there for drugs and the safest of safe sex—as an analogue for the whole of American (if not of Western) civilization. I found it equally easy to see the trio of whites—Rose, Red, and the young worker (again sucking one finger and the next, now on his left hand, now on his right, for any lingering taste)—as an analogue of whites and white culture up stores, the magic shop, souvlaki and hotdog and pizza stands, hardware stores, liquor stores, drugstores, cafeterias, coffee shops, and the second story rehearsal studios and the dry cleaners—the human services that, along the ground fronts of the two and three story buildings (now deemed wholly unprofitable for the Towering City), scattered among the porn shops, peepshows, sex palaces and fuck-film houses, once kept the area alive and livable for a considerable residence—have been boarded up or shut down.

"The crackers are drivin' out the cookies," has been the call on the street for a year, now. ('Cookie' refers to the bent spoon or bottle-cap in its hairpin holder—the cooker—with which heroin users traditionally boil up a fix, as 'crack' refers to the faint Rice Krispie crackle of the burning rocks as they heat to an orange within that American/Western complex. Perhaps the major appeal of the analogy was that the reversal, the subversion, the overturning of more usual analogical alignments of primitive and sophisticated, of white and non-white, initiated (at least momentarily) its own critique of precisely the failures of such racially analogic thinking (the overriding characteristic of the culture it symbolized) in the first place.

The kid watched the movie a few more minutes; finally he pushed his cock back into his jeans and zipped up. A minute later, he stood and wandered to the balcony door to go down.

"Man," Rose was saying to Red (she'd already said it now as many times as she'd said "Huh?" before), "what the fuck is he gonna come bother me for if he ain't got no money? That ain't right. I gotta get me some money.

glow in the screened-off end of the sooty glass tube through which the drug's inhaled.) But the crack trade, far vaster, cheaper, more visible, and more visibly damaging than the heroin traffic once was, is only part of the general decline.

This is the Strip: this is the neighborhood that, like numerous neighborhoods before it (Cannery Row, Farrell's or Bellow's Chicago, Runyon's Broadway) yearns to become a metaphor for the whole great American outside. There is no retreat/advance except within.

Rose was dozing in the ninth row of the balcony of the Capri porno theater on Eighth Ave. just below 46th Street, beside Red, one-time pimp, now wino and cracker, a scrawny guy with a medicine ball of dirty red hair, his winter-burned hands alight with the translucent bloat of the permanently undernourished alcoholic.

What does he think I am?" Still half asleep, Red was rubbing between Rose's legs now—his reparation for sitting beside her, offering what protection he can while she sleeps or works. "Man, what the fuck is he gonna come bothering me for if he ain't got no money, you hear what I'm saying..."

This interior?

All three whites there—or perhaps just the relationship between them (its cultural, analogical richness)—I found, on one level or another, sexually attractive: both guys physically so, Rose intellectually so. But that, of course, is where I find myself at the particular boundary of the everyday that borders the unspeakable, where language, like a needle infected with articulation, threatens to pierce some ultimate and final interiority—however unclear, as we approach it, that limit is (if not what lies beyond it) when we attempt analytic seizure.

Red was half asleep too, but now and again he'd scratch himself, pawing down inside the front of his jeans, clawing at his hip, bending to get at an ankle inside the double pair of sweaty tube socks I can smell from where I'm sitting a row in front of them to the left, now thrusting a hand through the neck of his sweater to rake out an armpit. Rose and Red were the only two whites visible among the young to middle-aged black and Hispanic men; here and there, long, forbidden flames from red, blue, and yellow Bic lighters, turned high and played along glass stems. The smell of the drug—a burnt plastic stench, beside which the spicy odor of pot seems healthy and organic—welled here, fell away there, or drifted across the flickering video projection at the front of the narrow theater.

Three rows down from Rose and Red a guy in a

The lack of clarity is, of course, what is there to be analyzed, articulated.

The unspeakable.

The unspeakable, of course, is not a boundary dividing a positive area of allowability from a complete and totalized negativity, a boundary located at least one step beyond the forbidden (and the forbidden, by definition—no?—*must* be speakable if its proscriptive power is to function). If we pursue the boundary as such, it will recede before us as a limit of mists and vapors. Certainly it is not a line drawn in any absolute way across speech or writing. It is not a fixed and locable point of transgression that glows hotter and brighter as we approach it till, as we cross it, its searing heat burns away all possibility of further articulation.

Rather it is a set of positive conventions governing what can be spoken of (or written about) in general; in black and white checked scarf with tassels was giving another guy a blow job, who leaned back staring through wire-framed glasses more at the ceiling than at the porn movie. Someone else was bending down between the seats, looking around with his lighter—and had been for ten minutes now—for any rocks that might have fallen on the floor between the cigarette butts and the soda bottles and the beer cans and the spit and the trickles of urine from the guys four and three and nine rows back, too lazy or too frustrated to go down to the john (which was always filled with five or six guys in the middle of a drug deal, anyway), and the dried and not-yet dried cum puddles. Someone else pushed his rolled screen from one end of his stem to the other with a wooden stick to collect the melted residues from the glass sides for another impoverished hit.

particular, it comprises the endlessly specialized tropes (of analysis, of apology, of aesthetic distance) required to speak or write about various topics at various anomalous places in our complex social geography—places where such topics are specifically not usually (or ever) spoken of: What is speakable between client and accountant is unspeakable between *newly* introduced acquaintances at a formal dinner party. (What about the unspeakable as a drug? Its history comprises laudanum, opium, heroin, and now crack. The unspeakable as drug becomes the epoch's romantic metaphor.) What is speakable between client and prostitute in the balcony of a 42nd Street porn theater is unspeakable between man and wife of thirty years. What is speakable between lovers of three weeks is unspeakable between best friends of a decade—and vice versa. What is speakable be-

The effects of the drug are kind of like a popper that lasts four minutes instead of forty seconds. Though it has no long-term withdrawal effects, it's got the worst come-down—between three and six hours of depressed headache, nausea, and achiness—this side of airplane glue. And its addiction schedule is fierce. Intermittent use over three months will hook you. And use on six consecutive days will make anyone an addict.

Someone else was moving up and down in his seat, quickly, rhythmically, shoulders shaking in a masturbatory frenzy. I'd passed him five minutes back: he'd pulled his pants off, balled them up, and put them and his coat in the seat beside him, so no one would sit next to him while he beat off.

In a man's down jacket clutched around her with folded arms, an anorexically thin black woman with miss-

tween a magazine essayist and an audience concerned with art and analysis is unspeakable between a popular journalist and an audience concerned with "everyday" news.

And there are a dozen people I—or you—might tell the story of Red, Rose, and the unnamed semenophage.

"Unspeakable," then, is always a shorthand for "unspeakable unless accompanied by especially pressing rhetorical considerations" (The unspeakable is as much about cruelty as it is about sexuality. Indeed, for many of us it is where they meet): I don't know how to tell you this, but...(The unspeakable comprises the wounds on the bodies of abused children, their mutilations and outrageous shrieking or tight-lipped murders at the hands of parents) I have something I really have to explain to you...(It is certainly any pleasure at such ing teeth leaned over me to smile: "You want company...?" Then, recognizing me for gay, she grinned, shrugged, and whispered, "Oh...!" and hurried on.

Oblivious, Rose opened her eyes. "Man, I'm itchin', too," she told Red: "You wanna scratch my back...?"

Red finished his own clawing and turned to Rose with a grunt and a couple of bewildered sighs. Without really looking up, he rubbed the side of Rose's navy sweatshirt.

"No," Rose said. "Underneath."

So Red put his hand under the frayed cloth and rubbed. Rose twisted in the seat. "Hard, man. Yeah, there. Hard. Like that. This is killin' me!"

Not looking any more awake, Red leaned his full hundred-thirty pounds (five of which is his hair) into her, rubbing, raking.

"That's it," Rose said, her back toward him. "Go on.

abuses, even private, pornographic, onanistic.) Allow me to make a special point here...(It's civil or political prisoners tortured or slowly slaughtered by ideologues or their hire.) You mustn't take it personally, but...(It is the uncritical conjunction in the mind of certain social critics of pornography and such pleasure—a conjunction that dissolves with any real experience of the range of current, commercial pornography or the real practices of practicing sadists and masochists—that makes the pornographic unspeakable, beyond any rhetorical redemption, impossible to apologize for.) Now, this may sound very cruel, but I feel I just have to say...

Quotability always allows, at least as a limit case, the everyday journalist to quote the unspeakable artistic and/or analytic text. (What he cannot do—what remains, for the journalist, unspeakable, save through

Keep it up, man."

In down jacket and knitted watch cap, another white guy pushed through the fellows hanging around the balcony door. Husky, good looking, between eighteen and twenty-three, he could be an apprentice starting at one of the construction sites further up, in from Long Island and just off work—or he could be a working-class student from one of the city's outlying colleges. Looking around the aisle, he made toward Rose and Red as only one white can seek out another in the dark sea. Sitting two seats away from where Rose still swayed under Red's rubbing, for a minute the new guy looked at the dull, near colorless picture down on the screen; now and again he glanced at the pair to his left.

Finally, he turned in his seat, smiled openingly, leaned toward rocking Rose, and asked: "Can you use another hand?"

an analytical raid among the esthetic figures of analysis, of apology, esthetic distance—is teased apart for his everyday audience the boundary, the gap between probe and presentation, between interpretation and representation, between analysis and art.) It is as if we must establish two columns, with everything of one mode relegated to one side and everything of the other relegated to the other.

It's as if we had to figure the impossibility of such a task, such a split, such a gap—figure it in language—rather than write of it, speak of it.

To speak the unspeakable without the proper rhetorical flourish or introduction; to muff that flourish, either by accident, misjudgment, or simple ignorance; to choose the wrong flourish or not choose any (i.e. to choose the flourish called "the literal") is to perform the unspeakable.

Not looking from under the bronze blades of her hair, Rose said: "Huh?"

"Can you use another hand?"

"Huh?" Rose still didn't look up.

"Can you use another hand?"

Rose looked now. (Red went on scratching.) "What'd you say?"

The kid was good natured, pleased with himself.

"I said, 'Can you use another hand?'"

Because there were new words in the sentence, Rose was back to the beginning of her befuddlement. "Huh?" She grimaced, with eyes already pretty much swollen closed.

(This much repetition is, of course, narratively unacceptable, aesthetically unspeakable: its only excuse is accuracy of transcription; its only meaning is the patient persistence of it: repetition, said Freud, is desire.)

The guy repeated: "Can

Many of us are not taught the proper rhetorical flourishes that allow us to say anything anywhere: How to tell your parents you're gay. How to tell your boss you want a raise. Having said any of these unspeakable things, that's no guarantee it will produce the effects we want. But the fear of reprisals (or failure) becomes one with the ignorance of how to say it. This is a form of oppression.

The history of the unspeakable descends most recently from the unprintable—from forties and fifties America when certain words would render a text "outside the law"—an interesting metaphor, as what the metaphor's exclusionary force actually once indicated was that, upon containing such words, a text became a privileged object *of* the law.

The metaphor was the underside of a system whose major thrust was protective. That which was within the you use another hand?"

"Huh?"

"Can you use another hand?" His tone of whispered good will did not vary.

Rose pulled herself up, tugged the front of her sweat shirt down (it rode up from her belly right away because behind her Red was still rubbing.) "You got any money?" she asked, finally, voice raucous and bitter.

The kid shook his head, laughing a little, not as a negative answer but just to acknowledge the suggestion's preposterousness. She can sell the niggers and spics around them ten dollar blowjobs, he was thinking, but not him. (Even he is unaware that Rose will go for five.) He turned back to look at the movie. Then, after another minute, he stood. Feeling along where foam rubber pushed between the metal backs, with their chipped maroon paint the color of his knitted cap and the torn corduroy of the

law—people, actions, texts, property—were protected by the law. What was outside the law was attacked, detained, impounded, exploited, and punished by the law. The boundary was between a passive surveillance in the name of protection and an active aggression in the name of retribution.

The notion that anyone should clearly and committedly believe in the absolute locatability of such a boundary is, for many of us (if not most of us), unspeakable. Yet we function as if such a boundary were lucid, absolute, and unquestionably everyday.

The everyday and the unspeakable are only the linguistic—the 'social,' in its most limited sense—shadows of this legalistic system: the passive surveillance and the aggressive attack of the law spoken of, written of, (figured) as an inside and an outside.

In many cases, desire lies

seat cushions, he edged to the aisle.

A few rows down, on the other side of the balcony, were three sets of two chairs apiece, all occupied except one at the front, before the iron balcony rail. Beside the free seat, in a black bomber jacket, fur collar up and white hair awry, an older Puerto Rican slept against the wall. The white kid moved down the aisle, looking left and right, like the eyes of a reader sweeping back and forth in their descent along the columnar text. (The unspeakable is always in the column you are not reading. At any given moment it is what is on the opposite side of the Moebius text at the spot your own eyes are fixed on. The unspeakable is mobile; it flows; it is displaced as much by language and experience as it is by desire.) Reaching the empty chair, the guy hesitated, pushed his lower lip over his upper a moment in thought;

like a bodily boundary between the everyday and the unspeakable. In some circles it is unspeakable to call men feminists: they may be "feminist sympathizers," but a "male feminist" is as much a contradiction in terms (as well as a sign of the most naive political co-optation on the part of any woman who accepts the term) as a "white black-militant." In other circles—American academe, for example—it is common parlance. In some circles it would be unspeakable to suggest that commercial pornographic films are relatively less sexist than the commercial non-pornographic cinema. Yet this is certainly the way in which they strike me. (However miniscule their plots, they have a higher proportion of female to male characters; they show more women holding more jobs and a wider variety of jobs; they show more but the Puerto Rican really seemed out of it.

So he sat down beside him and unzipped his coat.

Tugging his belt open (like a text that loops and seals upon itself, without commencement or termination, the unspeakable lies in the silence, beyond the white space that accompanies the text, across the marginal blank that drops opaquely beside the text toward a conclusionary absence that finally is not to be found), unsnapped his jeans, pulled down his fly, and parked his Reeboks on the lower metal rail. Tugging his cock out from the side of his briefs, he moved it from one fist to another and back a few times, before he began to jerk. From where I sat, across the aisle and a row behind, the head above thumb and forefinger looked like a Barbie-doll hardhat. His upward tug was clearly the business one; downward was just to get his fist back to

women instigating sex; they show a higher proportion of friendships between women; and they show far less physical violence against women than do the commercial films made for the same sociological audience. Their particular didactic message about the sexual act *per se* is that "the normal sex act" should include cunnilingus, fellatio, male superior, and female superior position; anything else is perceived as a diversion from this norm.) But it is precisely this rhetorical frame that makes such an analysis—here—speakable, precisely as it makes speakable the analysis of the sociology of pornography (in the literal sense of writing about prostitutes) that is to follow. The positioning of desire is a result of social power. But the content of desire does not contain—the way a mirror contains—social power, in image or where he could pull up. Now and again he'd rub the thumb of his free hand across his cock's crown to clear away the pre-cum leakage, raise his thumb to his mouth, and

in reality. (What it contains, if anything other than itself, is that tiny part of the freedom of language associated with abjection.) Indeed, it is

POLITICS

KATHY ACKER

the filthy bedcover on stage I'm allergic to this way of life mine? the last time I got on stage for the first ten minutes I felt I wasn't me I was going through mechanical personality changes and actions I got scared I might flip in front of the sex-crazy lunatics finally got into the Santa Claus routine I was a little girl all excited because Santa Claus was going to bring me Christmas presents I couldn't go to sleep I was waiting and waiting and then and then you know what happened doctor Santa Claus came right into my room I'm taking my clothes my shoes off rubbing my breasts Lenny dreamt last night about fucking Cyrelle she was lecturing him on how to fuck a woman he told her that he didn't need the lecture she thought he was wrong he was sucking an older woman's cunt it was also a cock without changing from a cunt this Is a romantic section a very romantic life ha ha I was writing in the projection room the shits said they'd clean and was the floor it's still piss black can't see no roaches no more it's hotter than usual the projectionist was constantly bugging me some guy they say drunk hit Josie on her ass during her show yesterday his hat the cashier says he came up told him you're not allowed to bring liquor up here then the cashier and Indian guy turns to Washington an old black janitor tells him that he's not to come again on the weekends he has no mind he can't remember anything he's not to ask to get paid again he gets $1.00 he's too old he won't be able to work much longer he's sick he's senile he's looking at me red blearing eyes   we're at the Embers cruddy food at least no one's taking off his clothes they all want to SCREW this week (we find in the projection room) is about orgies mentions every place but ours only the fuzz know about 113 swings SCREW says are very jealous about their mates? you can't get involved with a girl you fuck at an orgy unless you've got her guy's O.K. which isn't they say likely I don't know about vice-versa at an orgy everyone wants to have everyone else only once   no two guys together the males want to watch the females screw so that occurs it turns them on the best orgy I ever went to a cunt's writing started with two girls making it on the livingroom floor   Lenny tells me Lawrence is a romantic Kangaroo red and black striped overalls no hair I don't know what the fuck to do with it I'm getting to look so ugly it won't do anything like stand straight out fuss into balls two more shows and everything's over I felt dead writing before I could be dead now   waking up I got a sacred Mexican ring yesterday to do just that remember every single dream for the next two weeks as soon as I wake up not getting so pissed off all the time completely hostile   I'd like jewels this life's not romantic enough too hidden yet to be bound in the fucking brain and mind I have to get back to the show Lenny's putting on his coat son of a bitch

✣

I was a young wife last night I was scared that my husband took drugs you smoke a pot cold to sex unless I danced alone knowing that there were fifty other men in the red hotel room   I got really hot he kept taking too long blew him he ate me   the usual we still had time left so I danced naked Ike and Tina Turner's RESPECT he yelled at me to get on the floor in the doggie position I did immediately got up he said do it you're supposed to do whatever I say I did it looked up at him and went rrrf-rrf rrrrf-rrf the shits broke up I started crying again I want to go home to mommy you stupid cunt I want to see my mommy you're a brute I don't want to be married to you any longer O.K.   we'll go see your mother I like her too   Mark's good at being aggressive a tinge of nastiness they're sadists a good fit I worked easily except for the sex I felt weird with Mark couldn't get into it and fake coming I was more interested in kissing him or looking at his body   during the intermission I was talking to Ellen Mark and Mickey were making up she had done tricks for a while three times once a week went up to George Raft's hotel room he had an old-young travelling companion she fucked the companion turning Raft's sex the whole night Raft was nice to her she says told her that she should tell each guy she deals with why should you pay the pimp? agency? I don't remember anything pay me and I'll take the price down $10. she should also pick two or three guys she trusts to be nice and pay have them as private clientele not deal with strangers she was in a precarious position might get arrested beaten too large a cock and couldn't refuse alone in the room he knew one guy who got off on lying in a coffin and seeing the girl freak out   Mark comes up says that he thinks that no one if he didn't feel restrained would be normal weird ways of getting off Lizzy's licking Paul's ears his neck they're fighting with the ball hanging from the scratching post and kissing each other one girl he got so hepped up by his half lying said that she really wanted to blow a guy just as he was about to come for him to ejaculate over her face so she could rub it in a typical porno movie ending Mark repeated to her what she had said it was in a room of people she got uptight immediately left the room   I didn't have any trouble getting home Mark and Mickey walked me to the subway station so I could see if anyone was following me the D train came fast the AA I thought two guys were following me up 163rd but nothing happened Lenny and Hannah were asleep I hope Hannah's O.K. she's strangely quiet and in her room she might have killed herself she just got up I have to speak to her she's cold blaaah naah I was still jumpy wanted to rest eat some bread Lenny had woken up for a sec too conked out I tried to get Melvin worried by his letter the telephone was coocoo crawled into bed with Lenny but couldn't get to sleep for a few hours   this is the third dream sequence I'm not going to do anything for the next two days put down my actual dream an affair between me Mark and Lenny in the middle of the morning the joke about the rubbers: my daddy told me never to do it without a rubber whatever that is what are you talking about it's not raining the roof of the hotel room was leaking onto the gold bed long blonde fluffy hair over my cunt.

✣

Lenny won't call me La Mort he says he doesn't want to say a name that strange I dig the pun the whole day's been like this: we can't do the old show can't do any show except one which means something to us beyond the bread we make we probably should quit this fucking job the 12:30 show's gone a fuzz appeared about 12:05 saying that the theatre couldn't open until 12:30 the shits make up their own rules anything they crave syphilis wet cunt crap cock puss I Lenny says he'll call me the german for murder murderer? Morda that's better it'll be romantic I won't mind doing the show which is a really shitty show today but with the creeps males chauvinists rednecks pukes John Birchers worse liberals murderers we get in the audience it's a strong show they don't want to see anything but dead cunt they make everything dead with their eyes they're not going to dig any jokes they haven't for three months I come out dance strip do hard spreads no expression 10 seconds each held still to Ike and Tina Turner's RESPECT dance at the end sadism hands on the hip as they clap Lenny's the Shit Boss Mister Wolf call me Wolf that's real I have to fuck him to get the job dancing in his theatre my boyfriend's been busted etc. at the end I get the job of course we have to write a better 10-minute conversation about Bob Wolf I hate giving these fuckers spreads opening myself but we have to do the truth we might as well begin acting that way our romanticism a guy comes over here to use the sugar I jump Lenny asks if I got scared I'm always scared whenever now strange guys come over to talk to me   we see Mark and Mickey in the afternoon in the middle of the third show I say there's a friend of mine hello the only line the audience digs they're tripping more tea in my cup Mark stares at the stage lights my yellow socks and red and blue shoes I have to talk to Lenny   the Embers again confusion we have to speak loud and very distinctly because the lines are symbols real there ain't no conversation O.K. the audience digs the sadism bastards pimps every male's a pimp in this cruddy society caters to his lousy moneyed disease you get fed it from birth and can't get away except by severe disruption I'm a pervert a sneak I dig buying clothes nothing else the harder the cut the better I get confused about what people expect me to do I'm talking French today an Italian waiter asks me what I'm writing I start answering him in French Lenny says he's good looking I agree in my head but not turned on I never am I sound like I'm in the 50's not here on 42nd street I like people who say things I haven't heard before that's shit Mark was saying that he hates earning money he has to figure out how to maintain it living he's scared to walk around in the streets with money anymore he gives it to Mickey great solution Mickey laughing so hard he looks like he's an epileptic Mark's calling him she which is true they're getting deeper and deeper Mark wants to know if he's talking too loud he tries to be silent and actually is seven minutes he felt bad watching me on the stage all the shits cared about was my cunt they moved as I moved so they wouldn't miss a glimpse light meat they can't now he can't be around 42nd street he wants the bread to furnish his apartment acid doesn't last forever 100 tabs a day and an empty forest he'd be happy forever: the paradise I eat raw fish and chicken Lenn tempura and fish with soy sauce and ginger it's worth $13. half a dirty show the waitresses won't go near Mark and Mickey who are giggling like babies wanting to touch each other Mark says he likes Kall's dancing the best he'd like to work with her only she isn't as good with the audience as I am I feel hurt like the guy who told Lenny he didn't like my body then saw me sitting behind and ran like a frightened rat Mark's bluntness makes me easy around him I wouldn't commit myself to him in some dream or reality caused by a dream he and Mickey start saying that a woman should be subservient to a man it's only in America that women lead can lead the men around Mark's not a man he's not involved after chopping wood all day in the forest the man throws open the door of the cabin yells where's my dinner the woman cowers rushes to get it the vegetables not cooked right he throws her against the door we're all getting into it the restaurant's aghast take your clothes off wash my feet warm the shitting bed he'll throw her to the dogs howling in the darkness just beyond the closed door Mark says that if we took the bed offstage and substituted the low Japanese table Lenny could eat me with chopsticks oriental dish.

✣

had to go to work yesterday Josie's boyfriend Ralph got busted by the feds they broke down the door ripped the apartment apart T.V. bed furniture they arrested everyone in the place then waited for a few hours arresting everyone who buzzed the bell Ralph tried to escape so they shot him in the arm no one fixed his wound when he got to prison so he would have died if it hadn't been for the inmates $10,000. bail $5,000. had to be raised in cash. Josie had $1500.in the bank the feds took her bankbook so she couldn't get at the dough they didn't find the $2,000. hidden in the stove she's been going coocoo trying to raise the rest of the dough before they kick Ralph off he's going to skip bail as soon as he can he's been arrested too many times before she was going to prostitute Marty was in the theatre she told him Ralph had been busted what could she do to raise bail she'd do anything Marty said what for drugs? I'm not going to do shit for no drug dealer I don't want no drugs in this theatre he's not a drug dealer he's a psychedelic love-freak dealer Ken had told us on Christmas Marty gave him his $100. coke-snorters as presents Josie comes in every day sunk on barbiturates higher on dope Mark and Mickey are arguing Mark's pissed off he can't freely pick up anyone he wants to mainly guys some guy says to Mickey bye Mick Mark blows a gut how dare you talk to someone tell him your name you have no right to talk to anyone about our problems don't get the actors uptight blah blah he can't do the show anymore he wants us to do all of the work dance for 15 minutes seduce him when he comes on stage don't say a word god forbid he should have to think of a joke to crack I'm not going to take that kind of shit he makes the same money I do I tell him get someone else to do the show Ellen and I switch which isn't fair to Ellen but she takes shit all the time I get back for the 2:30 show Bob Wolf Big Shit Boss is standing in the back his hair's down to his shoulders to show that he's a hippy and loves everyone he wants to speak to me in an ominous tone I tell Mark start first what the fuck do you mean by almost quitting you can't walk out on a show I won't take that sort of crap I tell him very slowly controlling myself as much as possible to talk and not just to hit him I hate his guts so much the first and second shows on Sunday there's broken glass in the bed it's raining through the roof on the floor where I have to dance and on the bed so I'm working all day in sopping wet clothes and I'm overheated the rug's torn where I dance I keep tripping almost breaking my neck there's no music the place stinks the bedspread's turned brown it's so fucking filthy he starts screaming at me what right do you have to quit you just get out I don't need you you can't get out whenever you please I've tripled audiences on Sundays we've paid you we've never done nothing to you I'm going to quit unless you fix up that stage up in two weeks I'm not taking shit you've got my two weeks' notice get the hell out just give me notice get the hell out who are you to threaten me I'm not threatening you I'm telling you point-blank clean this turd fuck shit up Reggie came over last night he and Lenny were going to work for a few hours then we'd all eat dinner I got some wine and cheese for the moment Lenny was sitting on Reggie's lap kissing him they went into the bedroom Lenny told me Reggie said he didn't want to be alone with Lenny anymore Lenny called me could I come into the bedroom I had to peel vegetables but it could wait Lenny was reading a Paul Bowles' story a guy is hot for his son finds out his son's homo and blows a gasket they both go off to Havana I was lying beside Reggie smelling his skin and barely touching him I got into it really hot so I got up to go to the kitchen masturbate in a little privacy they all came in why'd you get up so I told Lenny I was hot for Reggie so Lenny wouldn't think I was bored with his reading Reggie seemed hurt I was talking in a low voice to Lenny I explained he acted nice kissed me we were in bed Reggie fucking me much you have to become a criminal or a pervert I'm in the bathtub touching the bones in my face I have no idea what I feel like I never touch myself except for occasionally masturbating a few times stick a finger up my ass hole or lick my nipple I draw my fingers around the back of my neck I want to shave my hair off again toes knees I admire criminals in my head knowing they're shits businessmen mother-fuckers like everyone else I don't want to fuck it doesn't mean what it should no one else thinks like this anymore I say angelic I'm sick of fucking not knowing who I am.

SAN DIEGO, CALIFORNIA, U.S.A. (1988)

WILLIAM T. VOLLMANN

Down in the golden grass near San Diego where houses and new houses terrified me, families lived the California life, saying to one another: If you can't feel it, never mind it. —A black lizard crawled and stopped. He heard what they said, and wanted everything to be true. —Like ants on rocks, bees among thorns, flies and then rocks, grass-shadowed rocks, the houses went on forever.

If only I could blow up the aqueduct, I said. Maybe that would stop them.

The lizard crawled and stopped. He heard me before I heard myself.

In the desert I hear the clink of climbing gear or the clink of rock before I hear the sloosh of water in my canteen. I never hear my own voice.

The lizard heard and didn't hear. He heard desert birds

talking to each other in long bright monosyllables.

Tomorrow I must die a little for your joy, the lizard said. He didn't hear his own voice.

Every time's a little drier than I remembered, I said. I didn't hear my own voice.

We both heard the slow double-beat of eagle wings.

The eagle saw cacti dead one day, green and blossoming the next. The eagle followed clouds like the branch-widening shadows of trees on narrowing rocks.

The grey dirt is covered with golden flowers, said the eagle. He didn't hear his own voice.

My voice was a bitter salad of Joshua tree flowers. The lizard's voice was a man's legs warmed by the sun through dark trousers. The eagle's voice was a long day.

Others were building new cities in the east, where life is blue space, where so many beaches and low dry mountains are overhovered by vultures. I heard the cities growing loudly. They grew like the voices on their radios, and cars made noise between them. Houses built themselves with hammering rackets. Garage doors hummed shut. Lawn mowers ate my scream. The lizard crawled under a house and said: You can study something for years and have no conclusion, but this is not to say you've gotten nowhere—He didn't hear his own voice.

The eagle said: This desert might look green if I fly high enough. —He didn't hear his own voice.

I saw a girl naked outside a house and said: You're too glowing to find meaning in but I can find meaning around you. —I heard my own voice.

She said: I can't hear you until you kill the lizard under my house.

I caught the lizard and said: I'm going to kill you. —He was screaming but I couldn't hear him. I killed him, and the girl and I poisoned his body together. We threw him on the road and watched. The eagle came to eat him and I said: You're going to die. —The eagle couldn't hear me, and I knew that and laughed. The eagle rose with the lizard in his beak. Then he screamed and the whole world heard. He fell out of the sky.

The feeling that I had to become something left me then, in that house where she and I always lived naked together. I knew that I was something, and did not feel trapped. Yes, I became something more evil and more good. Now that it is over, I can say that I was happy.

Once we went outside to look for lizards, but found none. We comforted each other, saying: Here will always be flies, will always be wind blowing until our ears ache.

THE WATER TOWER

JOHN BERGIN

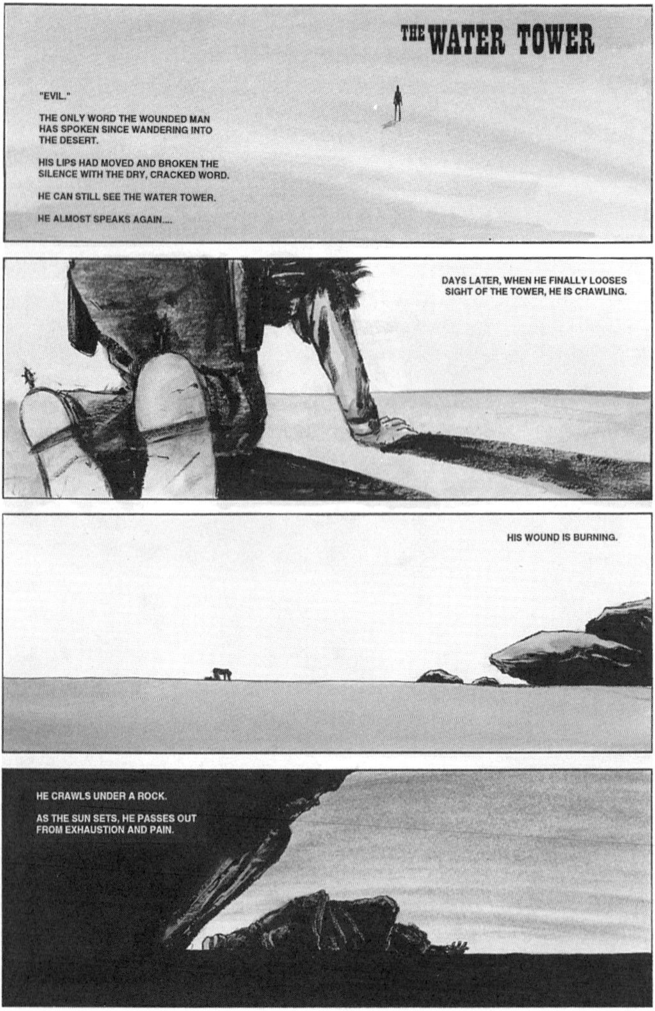
THE WATER TOWER
"EVIL."
THE ONLY WORD THE WOUNDED MAN HAS SPOKEN SINCE WANDERING INTO THE DESERT.
HIS LIPS HAD MOVED AND BROKEN THE SILENCE WITH THE DRY, CRACKED WORD.
HE CAN STILL SEE THE WATER TOWER.
HE ALMOST SPEAKS AGAIN....
DAYS LATER, WHEN HE FINALLY LOOSES SIGHT OF THE TOWER, HE IS CRAWLING.
HIS WOUND IS BURNING.
HE CRAWLS UNDER A ROCK.
AS THE SUN SETS, HE PASSES OUT FROM EXHAUSTION AND PAIN.

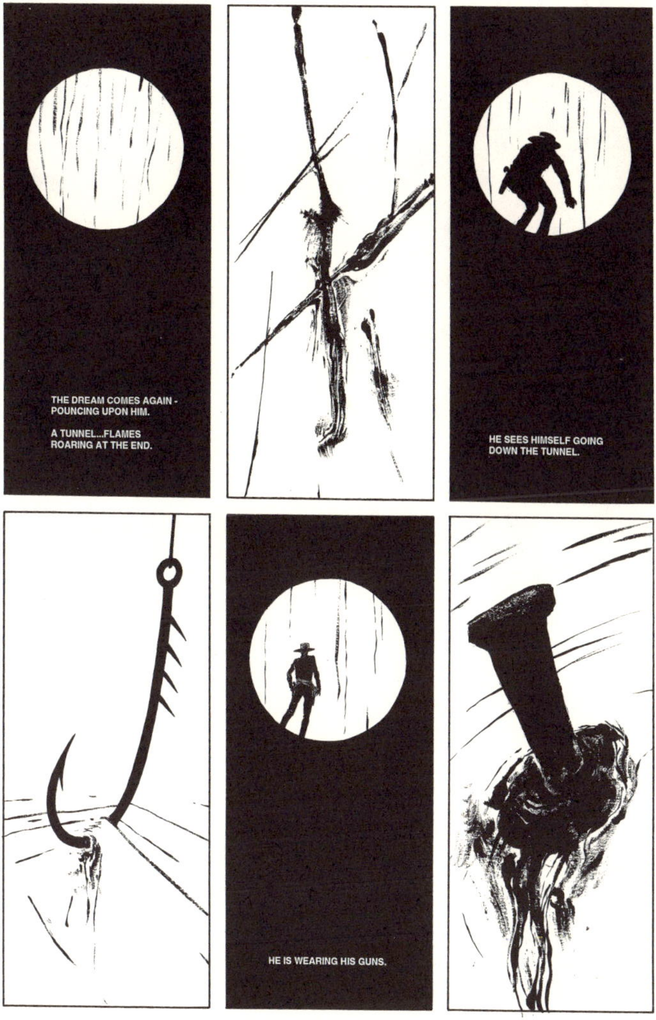
THE DREAM COMES AGAIN - POUNCING UPON HIM.
A TUNNEL...FLAMES ROARING AT THE END.
HE SEES HIMSELF GOING DOWN THE TUNNEL.
HE IS WEARING HIS GUNS.

THEY BECOME INSIGNIFICANT WHEN HE REACHES THE END OF THE TUNNEL...
HEAT TIGHTENS THE SKIN OF HIS FACE AND WATERS HIS EYES. FLAMES ILLUMINATE THE CAVERN AND DANCE OVER THE WITCH'S BODY. HER LAUGH FLOATS ABOVE THE WAILS AND SCREAMS OF PAIN. THE SOUND IS THUNDER. THE MAN SHE HAS CRUCIFIED LOOKS FAMILIAR... HE NERVOUSLY STEPS CLOSER, THEN FREEZES IN SPITE OF THE HEAT.
THE FIGURE ON THE CROSS WEARS HIS FACE!

help me.
YES. HELP HIM!

SHE SMILES AND ABSORBS THE BULLETS - ALL TWELVE OF THEM.
THE HANGING PEOPLE CONTINUE TO SCREAM AND MOAN...
THE SOUND AND EXPRESSION OF PLEASURE.
please... help me...
HE TURNS AND RUNS BACK INTO THE TUNNEL. HIS BREATH AND FOOTFALLS ECHO AROUND HIS HEAD.

SUDDENLY, THE TUNNEL IS BLOCKED
THE MAN FROM THE CROSS.
you should have helped me.

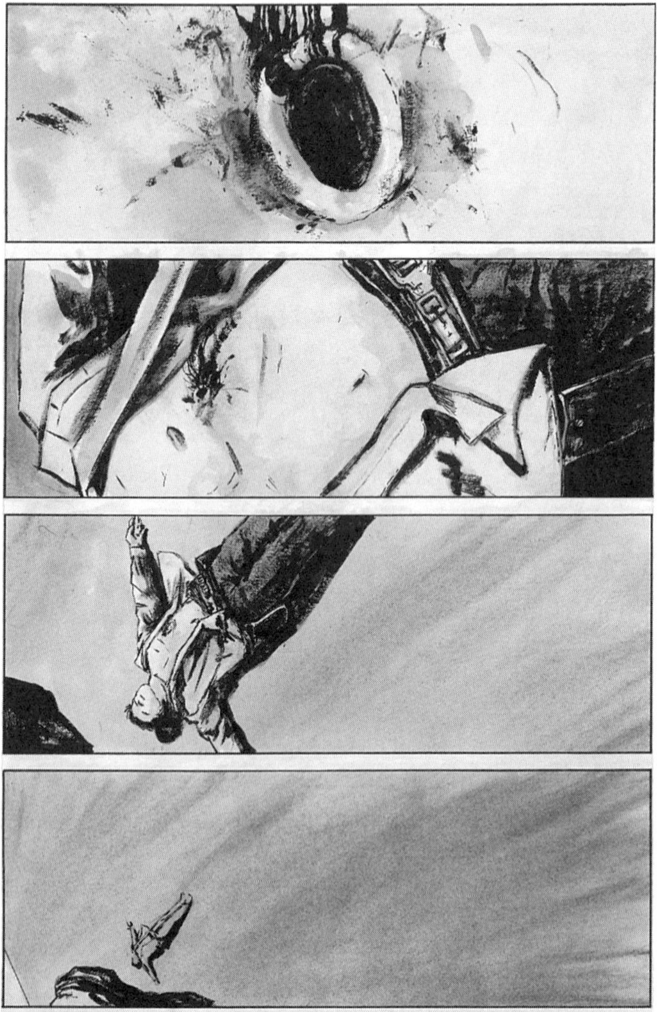

IT IS DAWN WHEN HE ROLLS OVER
AND BEGINS CRAWLING.

BY EARLY MORNING THE BUZZARDS
FIND HIM.

BY LATE MORNING
IT IS IN SIGHT.

BY NOON HE IS THERE.

THE WATER TOWER.
THE WOOD IS OLD AND BLEACHED WHITE. IT LOOKS LIKE BONE.
THE BURNING BODIES...THE WITCH...THE DREAMS...THE MEMORIES... THE WOUNDED MAN KNOWS THEY ARE THE PROPERTY OF THE WATER TOWER.
HE FINDS HIS HAT WHERE IT HAD FALLEN. HE RISES SHAKILY TO HIS FEET. ONCE AGAIN, HE RUNS HIS THIRSTY TONGUE OVER PARCHED LIPS. HE HEARS THE NAIL HE HAD DROPPED INTO THE WATER TOWER BEFORE. HITTING THE BOTTOM. WITH A DRY "CLINK".
THE SOUND ECHOES THROUGH HIS TEETH. MOCKING. EMPTY INSIDE. TAUNTING. NO WATER. LAUGHING.
HE SLOWLY CLIMBS THE LADDER MOUNTED TO THE SIDE OF THE TOWER.
BY LATE AFTERNOON HE HAS REACHED THE TOP AND CRAWLED TO THE OPENING WHICH LEADS INSIDE.

BY SUNSET HE IS INSIDE.
HIS BODY SAFE FROM
THE BUZZARDS, HE DIES.

CONSUMIMUR IGNI

HARRY POLKINHORN

It was 5 o'clock in the afternoon. Debord entered Alicia's, grateful for the cool darkness. After all, outside it was 117 degrees Fahrenheit. He sat in a leather-backed chair and ordered a margarita ("without salt"). The lime bit his throat as it went down. The gloomy interior of the De Anza Hotel's only bar helped him to concentrate. Debord had a lot to think about. People were dying a horrible death through convulsions and vomiting all over Calexico, and it was his job to figure out why.

Needle slid beneath skin. Rose burst back-up in the tube. Dark red silent explosion. TV flicker jump across nose eyes frowning brow. Idiom thieves. Invisible interior of formless. Slow-motion jolt to loosen bones from flesh afloat. Broken tooth of pain going away to dead. Sun mushroom against scarred horizon. Footsteps smell of salt cedar rank sewage burning agricultural waste hangs in air. Explosion of terrorist alphabet chunks across the screen.

He ran his fingers through thinning hair. His mind circled like a hound just off his scent, circled and back-tracked as if aimlessly yet well aware in its way, a calculated distraction, a meditation on nature, bestiality, beauty, the monstrous. The Calexico police had called him in because he had once had contacts with the Chinese Catholic group in Mexicali back in the 1960s. The local dicks figured he might be of some use in their deadlocked investigation. Whenever they couldn't do a quick make, they pinned it on the Chinese. Debord ordered another drink and ruminated. They didn't know about MIBI, and he wanted to keep it that way.

Debord's heart raced as he felt himself reaching a "plateau" in his mullings. He quickly paid for his drinks and went up to his room. Second floor, only room in the crumbling pile with a telephone. He unplugged the instrument and jacked in his portable computer. High-speed modem connect. Into the Internet highway and his code shot through the gateways to MIBI: Jorn in Copenhagen (Dotrement and Constant had fallen away, or rather been sheared off by developments too rapid for them to track), Pinot-Gallizia in Cosio d'Arroscia, Bernstein in Paris. "And me on the border, as usual," he thought sardonically. Lit a Camel and scrolled down to the relevant user i.d. numbers, knocked through a general call. He needed Giuseppe's knowledge of chemistry right away, and Asger's command of tongues. Bernstein would put the pieces together in her brilliant way. The gang moll but this one with a brain in her head. Debord was point man this time out. "Maybe you'll get some ideas for your next film," Jorn had chortled.

"Dozens of new cases are being reported each week," said Torres in a voice of barely controlled rage. "It's a goddam epidemic. We know nothing but what we read in the papers. The mayor and city council are kicking my butt." He glared around the office. Debord had his Sony minicassette recorder going in his pocket. Voice analysis later. MIBI procedures.

"How tight is the line?" asked Debord.

"We've got every dog in the house down there. The Border Patrol is cooperating so far. I spoke to Saldaña just before you got here. There are always leaks, maybe big ones, but the standard holes are plugged for now."

"Can you get me permission to go up into the water tower observation post?" Debord said. The Border Patrol had taken over the wooden gondola in the old water tower right at the fence.

"Sure." Torres punched up Saldaña again. "Pete. It's me again. Listen, Pete, I need to get my man up into the tower. O.K. Yeah, sure. I'll tell him. Thanks, Pete." He rang off and said, "You're in. A jeep will be by in 5 minutes."

The epoch itself is the frame of the whole work. How to plumb what could be an act of Chinese-Mexican terrorism. Beneath him the chain link and barbed wire stretched east and west. I wanted to speak the beautiful language of my time. To communicate and discuss. We grow older. Rose bomb in liquid, floats up through a dreamscape of all earthly things were corrupted. He looked through his binoculars. Here and there Mexicans slipped through holes in the fence headed north. Secondary details. At the beginning, I was nothing. His hands adjusted the plastic tubes, snapping everything into focus. The more profound is this desire. Violence, sexuality, cruelty. Turnings through a random city gridwork. A speaking voice proper only for suffering and despair. His 8-millimeter video unit patiently sucked in images. The huge sprawling metropolis to the south, sliced cleanly by the U.S./Mexico international boundary, in this case a fence topped with barbed wire, and on the north side the tiny town of Calexico with its neatly paved streets.

"Souls or bodies, what's the difference. The virus attacks life itself. Someone has unleashed a radioactive isotope that feeds on doubles. Is the soul the body's double?" The commander rose up on his toes, then rocked down, hands clasped behind his back. He looked intently out the window at the scene in the park across from the station. Swings, a merry-go-round, drunks asleep under the palms. Nothing out of the ordinary. A secretary handed him a fresh FAX. "Jesus, Mary, and Joseph," he swore. "Another rash of cases has been reported out in the Villa de Oro section of town. I'm calling the Center for Disease Control again."

Debord took this as his cue and left the station. He returned to the De Anza and within minutes was entering the day's catch into SI, a complex and beautiful program MIBI had commissioned. On a hunch, he flipped laterally out of SI into private notes, looking for the link: "On the evening of Dec. 31 in the same bar on the rue Xavier-Privas, the Lettrists came upon K. and the regulars terrorized—despite their own violent tendencies—by a sort of gang comprised of ten Algerians who had come from the Pigalle and were occupying the place. The rather mysterious story seemed to involve both counterfeit money and the links it might have with the arrest of one of K.'s friends—for narcotics peddling—in the very same bar a few weeks earlier."

"Bingo," whispered Debord. "Dope and the Lettrists." He slammed back into SI and ran the voice-print subroutine for everyone he had interviewed that day. Torres, Saldaña himself later on, and others. This took a while and the data were queued up in the buffer. Meanwhile he popped in master tracks for some radio programming from several popular norteña stations, then scanned in all the police stats the boys had given him. Once he had snapped the video conversion unit into its slot, the transfer was automatic. Before locking in with MIBI, he needed a break, because after they got started it would stretch him out thin.

Therefore the places most fitting for these things are church-yards. And better than them are those places devoted to the executions of criminal judgments; and better than those are those places where, of late years, there have been so great and so many public slaughters of men; and that place is still better than those where some dead carcass that came by violent death is not yet expiated, nor was lately buried...you should therefore allure the said souls by supernatural and celestial powers duly administered, even by those things which do move the very harmony of the soul...such as voices, songs, sounds, enchantments.

Girls used to put their belts, ribbons, locks of hair, etc., under the pillows of young men for whose love they craved.

Visible and tangible forms grow into existence from invisible elements by the power of the sunshine. This process is reversible by the power of night.

If a pregnant woman imagines something strongly, the effects of her imagination may become manifest in the child. The blood is magnetized.

Acting on a tip from a Mexican informant, Debord

nonchalantly entered the Copa de Oro. Chunks of the ceiling fallen away. A television monitor at each end of the short bar playing back grinding porno films. Nothing different from any other hole in the Chinesca. He sat at a tiny table and ordered a Tecate. One of those dives that featured only one kind of beer. Down to the basics. Soon the woman spotted him, as he had been told she would. Watch out for a set-up. Dark eyes lined with mascara, skin-tight dress of some white Spandex material, spike heels. He quickly scanned the joint, but no one seemed to care.

"Buy a girl a drink?" she asked.

"Sure. Name it." She ordered the predictable brandy.

"What brings you here?" she cooed, sliding a hand up his thigh.

"You," Debord said. "They tell me you know the new governor."

"Maybe I knew him," insinuated the woman. "I've known lots of men. Let's go to my room and I'll check my little black book." She tossed off the drink with one hand while massaging his upper thigh with the other.

"You're on," said Debord.

As he pulled up his zipper, Debord reminded the woman why he was there. She then said, "Sure, he used to come here. He liked me. We had some good times."

"Was he alone?"

"No. He always had several others with him."

"Any Chinese?" Debord asked.

"Yeah, as a matter of fact. I remember an older guy. Emilio Chin. They said he owned the Green Cat years ago and then got into the state gambling syndicate."

"How can I meet him?"

"Come back here a week from tonight at 11 p.m. I'll know

by then," she said, stuffing the bills into her bra. Then she smiled. "Come back any time, baby."

"By the way, what's your name?" he asked.

"Rosa."

Within 15 minutes Debord had walked back across the border and was in his room at the screen deep in SI. He ran the girl's voice from his machine, then a quick description of her features, clothing, and room. His i.d. began blinking: it was Giuseppe piping through with the chemistry figures. Blood sample analyses, projections of viral group activities, hormone cross-sections. SI reconstructed his voice which purred from the machine. "Your stats are flat on both ends of the curve," he said. "What kind of a place are you in anyway?"

"Somewhat isolated border setting," responded Debord. "They aren't much up on record-keeping here. It's all by word of mouth, gossip, chit-chat. But you do the best you can."

"Sure, Guy. Hang in there. Wait, here's Asger." The voice quality changed from a mild Italian to an even milder Scandinavian accent; SI did this just to make things more pleasant.

"Guy. Asger. Listen, I've done the full job on the samples. All the way down to the sub-phonemic level. You're dealing with some complex shit out there. My best guess is Mexican Spanish and third-level American on a bedrock of Mandarin Chinese. The diction subroutine tells us it's a woman between the ages of 28 and 34, educated through the equivalent of a 4-year college program, maybe in the U.S. Interests may be business, music, sex, and the occult. That's as far as I could get, Guy. She's smart and probably very dangerous.

Be careful, for Christ's sake."

Blip of static. Columns of figures filed across the screen, froze into a pattern, then disappeared as more came up, until the transfer was completed. He downloaded, ran his virus check, stuck a tracer block on the end, and broke the connection. 6:30 a.m. Suddenly he felt exhausted and stretched out on the uncomfortable bed. Too tired to care.

It was a critique of urbanism, of art and political economy. They operated through a series of turnings. Just as you felt you were on to something, they flipped the dial to another station. A twilight world of electronic haze as the ex-citizens watch "Dallas" over and over again. No one would be able to play because they would all be fixed in their allocated places. It was a question of premeditated memory control. Global marketing because of the lack of an overarching construction. This was the perspective: a shifting of tasks through negation itself force field sucks us into the now. Atomic fallout shelter against the fire storm of signs.

Over coffee and machaca in the De Anza cafe, Debord flipped over the pages of the *San Diego Union*. His eyes lighted on a headline: "Agreement said near on tighter controls over medical waste." His tour of the area had lead him to the conclusion that such concerns would be minimal here. "...trash from hospitals, clinics, and labs that can carry infectious diseases..." No one would think twice about unloading a pickup of plastic bags filled with such materials out on the desert or by the side of the road. After all, weren't the farmers themselves prime polluters of the food chain with massive doses of insecticides, fungicides, and herbicides? One would simply be following an example. So went his ruminations as he finished the spicy meat dish.

Later that evening, Debord kept his appointment with Rosa. "Any luck?" he asked.

"Sure. Chin is out of town, but his 'assistant' said she would meet us here. Look, here she comes now." The woman flicked her eyes towards the Copa's swinging half-door.

Debord turned to see. "Asger's right again," he said to himself as a Chinese Mexican woman of about 35 walked up to their table.

"Hello. I am Mr. Chin's assistant, Veronica Mah," she said in measured tones. "How can I help you?" Her skin had a deep glow under the dim lighting. She lit a cigarette.

"There's a big problem you might be able to help me with," said Debord carefully. He felt her scanning him with some Oriental power device. "My understanding is that the Governor, Mr. Ernest Appell, has some connections with, uh, certain merchandise crossing to the north...usually at night." He watched her expression.

"Yes," Veronica said readily, to his surprise. "I've heard the same." Pause.

"Well, to be frank with you, we need to know as soon as possible what the routes have been the last four weeks. Discretion assured, needless to say."

"Undoubtedly." Cold mastery of tone. Veronica was very accomplished. Debord was banking heavily on the locale. He figured she had done some kind of a check on him and probably had come up blank. Meanwhile, because of the isolation of this place the chances that she would deduce his distant team were very slim indeed. His recorder was trapping her in magnetic patterns. Veronica studied him through the smoke rising from her Delicado. He pushed an envelope across the table towards her. She pocketed it, rose, and left the club.

Back in SI, Debord uploaded all his fresh data. Then he rolled through the gateways to Bernstein. He needed her more than ever at this point. Getting in over his head. Her ability to make bizarre yet accurate connections would always help him see his way clear. She wanted to know everything about both women's appearance—makeup, clothing, color of hair, body shape, and so on. She asked about perfume, about the decor of the club, how he felt when he walked in, how he felt an hour after he had left. Then she said, "This might sound strange, Guy, but my suspicion is that these women are working together. They are playing Chin and Appell off against each other, and are probably doing the same with whoever owns the Copa de Oro as well as the local police commandante. What's in it for them? Control over their own destinies. Power over men, money. The Oriental is the brain, the hooker the contact point. Now, something went wrong with a big drug deal they were involved in, so they've come up with a way to implicate everyone but themselves, of course. Smokescreen. Think about it, Guy. And be careful, honey. I miss you." Fade-out with flashes of grey on the screen. The mini-speaker fell silent. Debord powered himself through SI's infinite recombinations, sucking in as much ancillary information as he could. Street and sewage systems maps of Mexicali and Calexico. History of the Chinese population in northern Baja California. Arrest frequencies by the Immigration and Naturalization Service, U. S. Customs, local police agencies. Cooperative agreements between institutions on both sides of the border. international law as applied to environmental issues.

Suddenly, a presence announced itself. For the first time,

SI had been breached. The screen went blank; then a complex mandala-like figure appeared in its center and began 3-dimensional rotations. "Mr. Debord," said a faintly metallic voice. "Please acknowledge."

Debord hit the "enter" key.

"Thank you. We have some information you may find of interest. Please join us at the Copa tomorrow evening." The spinning mandala then burst apart and disappeared like fireworks burning themselves out.

Because of Bernstein's suspicion, Debord was reluctant to involve any police agencies. The dicks would probably turn on him. He had to go in alone, therefore. He quickly reviewed MIBI procedures for such situations, then entered the club. Both women were there having a drink. He noticed nothing unusual as he approached them. "Good evening, ladies," he said. "May I join you?"

"By all means," said Veronica. "Yes, you are right; we requested your presence here tonight. We have a business proposition for you, Mr. Debord." Debord's biological and electronic systems shot to total alert.

"Please go on," he said calmly.

"A simple exchange. We give you the information you need, and you provide us with a clean copy of the SI program with all its subroutines. Really quite impressive, what little of it we were able to experience."

"You surprise me," confessed Debord carefully, concealing his real surprise. "SI permits very advanced research." He gestured around somewhat vaguely at the dilapidated surroundings.

"Yes. Well, then, do we have a deal?"

"Of course," Debord said. "Since you know enough to

have cracked SI's crystal wall, you will have learned that operators can send clean copies at their discretion. I therefore suggest that we conclude our arrangement later. Since my time here is limited, I would much prefer to spend it in more enjoyable pursuits." Veronica nodded, smiling.

"Agreed. And now I'll leave you." She extended her hand. "It was a pleasure meeting you, Mr. Debord." She turned and was gone. Rosa's fingers crawled up his thigh.

While walking back across the line, Debord worked out his strategy. First he knew that he could not communicate with the others at this point. Also any further browsing in SI would undoubtedly be monitored and deciphered. They would be aware of any moves. With this in mind, he returned to his room at the De Anza and packed his equipment. It was 2:30 a.m.

Debord carried his bag down the back staircase, which gave out onto the small stage on the east end of the huge lobby. A musty stage curtain concealed his presence. He waited until he was sure no one was in the lobby, then slipped quietly out the side door, which enabled him to make his way to the parking area. The taxi he had ordered was waiting.

"Travelodge, El Centro," he said. Thirty minutes later he was jacked into SI and immediately constructed a fog macro to give himself some room to maneuver. Debord uploaded one last time, ran all the relevant subroutines, then pulled out for a breather. "Time to close this case," he muttered to himself.

With that he dissolved the macro. Almost instantaneously they were there. "Are you ready?" asked Veronica.

"Yes," said Debord. "I've constructed the syntax which

will permit you to pull a clean copy of everything off the Paris node. This is the only one we are permitted to use. Gateway codes, user i.d.s, everything you'll need is in the file titled 'Situation.' Now please reciprocate."

"Of course," Veronica said. "Appell burned Chin on a large cocaine shipment." Bernstein was right again, Debord thought, smiling. "So Chin set him up by infecting the local branch of the state blood bank with a virus. He made certain that a transborder shipment destined for the Calexico Hospital was dirty. Appell is due for a fall. When Chin returns the blood bank and governor's office will be indicted. That's how these brutes operate. Rosa and I, however, knew the Calexico police would be baffled and that they would call in help. Of course we had heard of MIBI but had had no direct dealings. Your methods are very admirable. With SI now you can run back the virus."

"Why have you told me all this?"

"For our own reasons, we are pulling the plug on Chin and Appell. They've used us for the last time. SI will make it possible for us to break free, finally. We are tired of all the violence and dying. Good-bye."

Debord quickly logged off, whipped his equipment back into its carrying case, and left the Travelodge running. An explosion rocked the wing he had exited before he was across the street.

The bourgeois epoch which wants to give a scientific foundation to history overlooks the fact that this available science needed a historical foundation along with the economy. What hides under the spectacular oppositions is a unity of misery. All aspects of technology serve to produce the greatest possible passive isolation of individuals as well as the control of these individuals. He raised the glass to his lips as the others waited. Glad to be back in the Latin Quarter. "A toast to MIBI." They all clicked their glasses. Letters blossomed on the screen. Filter. The instrument of enchanters is a pure, living, breathing spirit of the blood codes. Robbers of language. The kind of knowledge that one ought to possess is not derived from the earth nor does it come from the stars. A destiny more grand than anything imaginable. Mystic flesh rose of finished passion traceries staining a bruised sky. Body parts. Political theory river running with by-product. Return.

Calexico/Mexicali
1990

WINGO ON THE SANTA MARIA

GERALD VIZENOR

The Santa Maria Casino opened in international waters on Lake of the Woods. The seasons turned and tribal winters were never the same on the reservation. Two Ministers, for instance, the old man who lies that he is more than a hundred and seventeen years old, taught his two mongrels how to howl "wingo, wingo, wingo," when someone shouts "bingo" at the casino.

One by one the tribal elders turned from television that summer to hear the wild sound of wingo numbers. The few players who won heard trickster summers in the spring, and even the losers overturned the seasons with their best stories. Bingo, believe it or not, became the new moccasin games on the reservation.

Stone Columbus, a native son from the reservation, owned the bingo casino on the barge and made a fortune in four seasons on games of chance. Not in the winter with trickster stories, as his envious critics have contended, but in the heart of summer when white tourists were eager to gamble on their vacations in northern Minnesota.

The Santa Maria Casino opened on a houseboat and then moved to an enormous barge near an island on Lake of the

Woods. Stone brought his family into the bingo business. Binn, his grandmother, a collector of boxes, heard that a "casino on the water is as much a reservation as a canoe in the wild rice, so lake bingo and lucky rice are outside the state gambling laws." Indeed, the casino was a chance reservation, a word and number game on water, the very first of its kind in the tribal world.

The floating casino was a sensation the instant it opened that summer. Television focused on romantic rebirth of the lost tribes, and three feature stories on the unusual genetic theories of the crossblood founder of the new casino on a barge. Reporters liked to hear the muskie shaman talk about how he traced his descent to the great adventurer Christopher Columbus.

"The red bloods returned to this continent more than a century before the blue bloods arrived the first time on the Mayflower," he told a reporter for the *New York Times*. "Histories have changed, and now some tribes trace their blood back to the Santa Maria."

Stone posed on television but he would never speak to cameras. He agreed, however, to be heard on national radio talk shows. He was raised on radio late at night, and learned how to hear and imagine the stories. Those late night talks were discoveries of the outside world and the sources of ideas on the reservation.

Stone trusted the radio, he trusted what he heard and could imagine late at night, and he raved about silence, waters demons in the stone, sarcastic humor, and fancy dancers on the Fourth of July. He could hear voices in cold rooms, and in the back seats of abandoned cars on the reservation. He was not a reservation trickster then, not a serious man with a vision of the past, but he was a natural muskie shaman on the water.

Binn Columbus shouted that her grandson was a shaman because he could "remember everything he ever heard on the radio." She cocked an ear to a row of boxes near the window and told stories, the past histories of the containers. She hears voices in containers, hollow trees, weep holes in bones, and panic holes on the meadow.

Two Ministers remembers the most stories on the reservation. Binn, he said, heard his secrets once when he fell asleep with his mouth open. She has been asked by many people to reveal the secrets from open mouths, but she refuses to be the tribal eavesdropper for suspicious husbands, wives, and lovers. The very idea that she could hear the past in silence was worth more than the loose thoughts she might have overheard in a yawn. Whatever she heard in holes and containers was all the more believable because the muskie shaman could regenerate body parts with imagination and miraculous genes.

Stone was heard that summer by millions of people late at night on talk radio. The crossblood of the northern air told stories that would soon transform memories, the origin of the tribes, and the genetic state of the nation. As he spoke from the bridge of his bingo barge, thousands of people circled the casino in canoes, power boats, and float planes from the cities. The people came to gamble on a floating reservation. They were white and on vacation, urban adventurers who waited on the water to lose at bingo, cards, and electronic games of measured chance.

"Admiral Luckie White is on the air once more, your late night host on Carp Radio." The radio was heard in four directions on enormous loudspeakers over the mast. "Stone Columbus is back with your answers and mine. Here we go once more in the dark, so, do you expect our listeners to buy the story that your brother is a stone, a common rock?"

"Stone is my name, not my brother, and we are not common," said Stone. His voice was rich and wild, a primal sound that boomed late at night over the lake. "The first trickster stone is my totem, my nation, there are stones in my tribal families, and the brother of the first trickster who created the earth was a stone, a broken stone that has landed everywhere on the earth."

"Really, but how can you be a stone, a real stone?" she asked and then paused for a outboard motor commercial. The talks from the casino two or three times a week had attracted new listeners and, to the everlasting pleasure of the radio station owners, new advertisers. The muskie shaman and his stories had saved the station from bankruptcy.

"Stones hold our tribal origins and our words in silence, in the same way that we listen to stories and hold our past in silence," said Stone.

"Stone Columbus, our listeners know you were born on a reservation, and we understand how proud you are to be an Indian, so how can you claim to be a direct descendant of a stone and Christopher Columbus?"

"Columbus was Mayan," said Stone.

"You must be stoned," she said and laughed. Her voice bounced on the water and the boats rocked with laughter near the casino. "Really, you must be stoned on that reservation boat, how can he be Mayan from Genoa?"

"Columbus was here on the great river, he was an adventurer in the blood and he returned to his homeland," he announced from the bridge of the Santa Maria Casino.

"His homeland, now wait a minute, this is serious."

"Stories are always serious," he shouted.

"Mayan genes, are you serious or what?" asked Luckie.

"The truth is in my genes, we are the tribal heirs of the great explorer, and he was here with us looking for gold and tribal women," said Stone.

"So, what did he find?"

"Samana, the golden tribal woman."

"Now we get the real story."

"Samana is a blue shimmer," said Stone.

"Stone, wait a minute, you leap from stones, to genes, to blue tricksters, and back again, so take your time now and spell it out in your own words to our listeners," said Luckie White.

"There was a stone shaman sailing near the islands."

"Was she the Mayan?"

"Mayans were much earlier," said Stone. "About five hundred years ago the stone shaman encountered three ships and many strange men from the sky."

"White men from the sky?"

"The white men from the sky were searching for gold and my stone relatives told them how to find it," said Stone. The gamblers on the nearby boats shouted to the bingo trickster, "Show us how, show us how to win the gold." Stone waved to them from the bridge. "Wait your turn and come aboard to take a chance," he told them over the radio. The mongrels barked, "wingo, wingo, wingo."

"So, what did the stone say?"

"Search for gold at the source of the great river."

"What river?"

"The Mississippi River."

"Fool's gold, that must be the punch line, right?"

"Christopher Columbus listened to our stone stories and then he dreamed the river, he dreamed tribal women, and he dreamed that his heirs wore golden masks," said Stone.

"But you said stones were silent," warned Luckie.

"Stones are silent, stones are the hand talkers."

"Columbus lost his hands, and other parts, right?"

"You see, the first tribal people who encountered the great explorer could not hear, they were deaf, a silent tribe of wanderers who spoke with their hands," explained Stone. "Because they were silent they could tell stories with their hands in the summer."

"Hand over hand, so to speak," said Luckie.

"Tricksters are the worst hand talkers."

"Stone, you lost me there with the hand talk stories," said Luckie. She teased the muskie shaman over an aspirin commercial. "Carp Radio is back to take calls, questions, and comments from our listeners."

"The hand talkers are blue," said Stone.

"Columbus was a Mayan, what about that?"

"Jesus Christ, Columbus, and Sephardic Jews are crossblood Mayans," said Stone. "Mayans were the great explorers, and they settled in the Middle East." His voice was wild and bounced on the water and turned the cattails. "Jesus was a shaman, and he traveled out of his body. Christopher Columbus was a dreamer too, and he found his homeland at last."

"Albuquerque, what's on your mind tonight?"

"Mayans, man you must be crazy."

"Saint Louis, go ahead with your question," said Luckie.

"How can you tell when you got the right genes?"

"Columbus carried our genetic signature in the stone, and we hold the chemical code that proves we are the heirs of the great explorer, we got the secret in the stone," said Stone.

"You told me, so how can it be a secret?"

"The Ghost Dance Genes are the secret, the seventeen gene signature is the tribal secret, and that secret is mine, held in the stone, but soon you might hear about the power of our healer genes," said Stone.

"Luckie White has the last word, and the last word tonight is in the stone," she announced and then paused for a commercial. "Carp radio ran the wire once more, hear you real soon on those late night voices of the truth."

The Santa Maria Casino was decorated with spirals of colored lights and a huge square sail that flopped in the breeze; two tribal women danced in a crow's nest above the mast. Four tribal medicine poles and an enormous spirit catcher loomed over the bow of the barge to protect the new reservation from natural water demons and disasters. The catcher held a blue light that night, and boats passed in the mist.

Stone wore a scarlet tunic and steered his casino in wide circles on the lake. Each turn, he calculated, was worth more than a thousand dollars. He saved millions of dollars in four summers on the casino. In the cold winter, tribal elders were bused from the reservation to the barge at the island dock. They praised the ornate interior, the solid birch tables in the casino, ate a free lunch, and then told their stories.

At the end of the fourth summer the casino was struck by lightning in a thunderstorm. The catcher turned over, the sail burned, and the rusted bow burst. The barge sank in shallow water on the international border near Northwest Angle.

Stone continued his stories on talk radio from the remains of the casino. His bingo investments, bonds and notes, matured and earned him more than a hundred million dollars. He created a new tribal nation with the cash from the casino and established the genetic research laboratories at Point Assinika.

OKAY WITH YOU?

RICHARD MELTZER

If you wanna kill me, and I know you do, stick my head in a cube of concrete four-foot square with two tiny airholes, just enough to breathe, and dump me out a chartered 707 seven miles above Lake Huron: sploosh! Or slice me with a guillotine the long way, from the scalp down, just in front of the ears, alongside the eyes, so I bleed 360 degrees with my face intact on sidewalk, lips kissing cement—I *love* cement (love it!) almost as much asphalt. But if you can't find a professional model imported from France, try this: cold kiss of concrete scraping *fuck* out of my nose, eyes, cheeks, teeth, and don't forget the chin. Drag me with an anvil on my head as skin, cartilage and stubble from my beard become food for roaches, y'know the *large* kind, or here's an idea: drown me in Elmer's Glue. Elmer's in my nostrils, eye sockets, throat, or just shoot me in the face, whole face, close range, couple feet at most. A shotgun—make sure it's loaded—would be fine, okay. Okay with me if it's okay with you.

DAYS OF BEER AND DAISIES

RICHARD MELTZER

I haven't been a raving drunk since nineteen...eighty. Drunk often yes—but not raving.

Duh *da* da da duh *da* da, duh *da* da like you, duh *da* like you do, duh *da* da duh da. Duh *da* da da duh *da* da—NAME THIS TUNE—duh *da* da your name, duh *da* so ashamed, duh *da* wasn't you, *wasn't you,* and then the chorus, YOU ARE, well it can't be anything but, you got it, "You Are Everything" by the Stylistics. You are everything and EVERYTHING IS YOU. I used to sit and *weep* over that one, weep at the sentiment, weep in goddam *awe* at the notion of YOU as essential principle, as *the* essential principle, every bit as basic as Thales's water, Anaximenes' air, Pythagoras's number. I never bought the record or heard it on radio, only way, only *time* I ever caught it was of jukes in bars. I'd be hunched over a drink as it played, ruminating only *occasionally* over a specific you, past or present, an actual second-person other, and depending on how much I'd already had, by song's end I'd be either a mawkish/maudlin mess or *sublimely* mawkish/maudlin...you had to be there to see it.

A case of camaraderie. Mike Tonk and I, who for years had been scribbling paragraphs for the same youth throwaways, finally met at a luncheon for the British band Grudge. Second thing he said to me, bourbon in hand, was "Let's go somewhere and *drink*." It was one-deep at the bar, maximum wait couldn't have exceeded a minute, everything was free but okay, *let's*. We found some place on 10th Street where the average age was 80, drank shots and beers till they closed at four, and became great friends—continuing to drink together, greatly. Never drinking buddies in the normal sense, we were more like colleagues on a fervid inquiry into drink as means and *content* of revelation, each encouraging the other to be perpetually drunk (and sometimes write about it). Though the *Village Voice*'s response to a proposed "In Whiskey, Veritas" column was decidely cold, we contributed essays on liquor by brand (Harper's, Old Crow) to the *New York Squeak* and *Boston Subgum*.

"What is scotch?"—we'd talk like that, get real theoretic. The answer, we decided, was *Scotch is an odd experiment in nu-drink, roughly equivalent to dropping a cigarette in Irish whiskey, as close (in its way) to Drambuie as it is to pure intoxicant.* Purists, we abhored admixture. Other options open, mixed drinks never passed our lips. Piped Mike when offered one: "Bottled booze is *already* mixed—mixed with water." Tough guys, we were tough. So tough that one night, for the fuck of it, we hit an East Side biker bar with mixed drinks our goal. Beginning with Carstairs & tonics, we moved on to sidecars and bourbon Manhattans, then ordered a single Zeus (vodka, Campari) and a blood & sand (gin, sloe gin, crushed ice). "How's that again?" asked the harried barman. (Fortunately, en route, we'd torn pages from a mix guide at the Strand.) Lacking both essentials, he couldn't make us a 252 (151 rum, Wild Turkey 101), so we improvised a 240 (Seagram's V.O., Christian Brothers brandy, Juan Valdez tequila, 80 each). We didn't even *ask* for a Rasputin (vodka, clam juice, anchovy-stuffed black olive) but were on a collision course for applejack highballs when, at pool, I lost our last five bucks to this old guy with one eye sewn shut. Hangovers: no worse than usual.

Four Tuesdays at Lynch's. We're invited, me and Mike, to this taproom in the West 50s, Lynch's Cafe. "You'll love it," says Jim Sibley, an earnest urban fellow, "it's an *Irish bar.*" (Ooooh hey not too many of *those* in New York.) Venue for a conclave of "some fine, nice writers," Jim included, a weekly "literary lunch." Invited, we go: a middle-middleclass bar. You couldn't be more middle. Sanitized, polished, service too polite, cardboard food. We meet the regulars: hi hi hi hi hi hi hi hi. From *Esquire, Women's Wear Daily, Newsweek, Cue.* A freelancer named Jane who's just interviewed Buckminster Fuller for *Vogue*. Jim covers fires for the *Post.* White-collar jackjills whose collars really are WHITE. A round of martinis? Mike and I will have beers. As gents who when we write (dine) (play) get at least *something* on our collars, faces, souls, we rise to the chore of showing 'em how it is done. "This porkchop is *shit.*" "Did you ask Bucky if he can still get it up?" "Garçon!—TWO MORE." (Cold stares from Jimbo, from the rest.) Next week, attendance down, we bring a pint of Soul Bros. blended whiskey. Jim, who any stiffer would be uncooked spaghetti, begs us: "*Please* don't let old man Lynch see that." Agreeable to a fault, we keep it bagged, pass it under our seats. Under the table we empty water glasses, piss in them—why interrupt *dialogue* in pursuit of a pot? Third week (more no-shows) we bring meatball heros. Fourth week we're the only ones there.

Solo fright. I used to be SHY with the women. Alcohol has played a role in two-thirds (three?) of my first-date insertions. Alc. in *me*, probably them too, though you'd have to ask them about them. Even minor doses have made my fool's twaddle smoother, my pawings less awkward, my idiot heart-thump less conspicuously LOUD granted my auto-meatpilot license to extemporize, to *dare*, handed my undiapered hormones the keys to the bank...rendered my rawest, crudest o.k.-let's-*fuck* palatable (even "charming"), painted my bottomless hunger wholesome and "natural," helped reveal me as an oft-tender fun guy with a joyous predilection for the BOY-GIRL PLAYPEN—playground—play house. The gift of play: nothing to sneeze at. Play at some point *declined*, howev (and intake continued) what exactly do you do with all the rocket-fueled idiot momentum, idiot frustration, idiot id?

She slammed and locked the bedroom door behind her, permitting my free reign over the balance of her feet. Singing "Some Enchanted Evening," I found and uncorked her last remaining liter of Sauvignon. With a black felt-tipped marker I scrawled "KIKE KUNT IS GOOD KUNT" on the inside rear of the fridge, pausing to whack off in a wide-mouth catsup, and the underside of a faded Eastern rug. Switching to blue, I drew swastikas on select pages of *Jonathan Livingston Seagull* and the inner sleeves of Bob Dylan, Bette Midler and Carole King LPs. Before departing I slipped a clump of pubic hair in a jar of skin cream and—be my Valentine?—dropped the last roll of Charmin in the bowl. Love and wine. Wine, love, truth. Truth and love.

"There are things drunks do that alkies don't," Mike would sometimes, while still lucid, claim. He'd go up and down one of those checklists of alcoholism, the 37 "warning signs" or some such, and take care to distinguish the alcoholic from the drunk. "Alkies don't," said this man who was both, "they *usually* don't fucka your mom. But honestly, man, who fucking *cares* if you 'drink before six' or 'one beer is never enough'? 'Has a cocktail while reading the stocks.' What it all comes down to is either you are or are not someone who drinks all the time. If you're not drunk every day, why bother? You're *wasting your alcoholism*, which is something a real drunk would never do."

47, 48...where's my drink? 49th floor, overlooking the U.N. Something on the rocks. Where'd...then I realize it slipped off the window, the ledge, I *remember* having pushed it with the heel of my hand. Nobody saw me. I believe no one saw. But nothing in its line of descent could still be breathing. A headline overwhelms me: "Party Reveler Beheads Diplomat"—though impact would also (I hazily guess) 've shattered the glass into fragments too small for i.d. At sunset I'd spit over the edge and watched my saliva break up and scatter...could my *ice cubes* just now have done likewise, slaying half the Finnish delegation? I look down—too dark to detect signs of life and/or death...but definitely no ambulance.

Another night, another trance. Closing time plus 15 minutes. Tired of ripping wipers off taxis, bending antennas, stuffing dead mice in gas tanks—*normal* vandalism—we're strolling down 14th St., me and Mike Tonk, when whuddo we see but this huge potted *shrub*. Some kind of budding, flowering thing—not a fern, not a rosebush (no thorns)—daisies? A rose in Spanish Harlem, a daisy—petunia?—begonia?—on scuzzy 14th. Freshly installed, *healthy*, it don't belong here nohow: what to do? "Kill it!" shouts

Michael, "KILL IT!" Great idea. With my full weight I dive at the thing, tackle it—no resistance, snap, *take that.* Funny funny. Next thing we know these cops're after us, running up stairwells, a door?, locked, nowhere to hide, gotcha. One cop holds us and I'm panting, thinking *what sentence*, what is the *music* you face for shrub abuse, six months in Sing Sing, a year? For parole you buy a new shrub, two shrubs, then they force you at gunpoint to pot them? Then his partner comes back w/ the drunk who turned us in—too drunk to recog our faces or clothes. "N...no. N...no"—lucky us, lucky me. BUT I DON'T EVEN *MIND* GREEN THINGS THAT BUD. (I didn't drink again for a week.)

WHAT IS THIS THING CALLED NIGHT?

RICHARD MELTZER

WHAT is most knowable, IS. Plato said that. I dunno most, but how 'bout the converse—what is least knowable, most unknowable, ain't? Dunno that either.

THIS much I do know: darkness isn't dying. (I will not die at night.)

Night sweeps noTHING from the table. "The hand, as dealt," she CALLED to say, "remains unchanged, unshuffled: a three-card flush, a pair of shit in hell.

"NIGHT is paltry life everlasting: everlasting *this* life now."

DREAMS OF A MIND RUPTURED PRINCE AND MOUTH PLAY

DAVID MATLIN

Up around Chalk Bluffs near Bishop there's a petroglyph. Once in a while Tom'd throw a row boat in the back of a truck and drive. Usually this was the one stop between Arlington and Mono Lake, especially if there was gonna be a rash of A Bomb tests. He'd just row out in the middle of those salt flies, and wait to see one of the poisoned flashes against the top of sky. Take a survey of what he thought was protection or at least what he thought about it. He liked the middle of the lake for that. The way it could streamline what the strange abstract scratches in the rock said about being human and the superimposition of the demented X-Ray that Tom was trying to experience personally upon the earth and sky. The terrible emergency that he knew didn't have a button or an alarm or even a goddamned squeak. If he was in the rose fields some nights he could even see the glow of the burning B52 fuel that'd sat too long and got rotten. Fuel at least that would never carry one of these Death Giants to its appointment. The flames and smoke-reek were part of the delicacy of the feast where any morsel might instantly go into decay.

Often the rose fields were the receivers too of the B52 mid-day shadows, the fields swelling with that darkness as the pilots, practicing for their final below radar extinction runs, would wave at Tom through their radiation proofed cock-pit glass.

He remembered one particular man, who came often to the farmer's parties. A Korean who'd had this job walking in the posh commercial section of San Francisco at noon dressed in a pink rabbit suit with floppy ears and a little furry tail to advertise some business. He'd gone to college. Wanted to be an architect. Except he'd had this other life in Northern Maine. Clear from Hollywood where his mother had been the only Korean starlet circa the nineteen thirties this side of a thousand hemispheres and the oceans that might separate them. He was way over six feet and not quite able to figure out his presences under the eucalyptus and palms even though America'd fought a police action where his mother and all her mothers before her had come. The Korean War was the same to him as a Nevada A Bomb Test just another x-ray wandering off a screen or a planet with a forgotten name. He enlisted in the Air Force after High School. Went East. Flew out every few nights in a B52 and its last of the species contingent. He held the key. The flight and crew were the ornaments that got him to the electronic edge of the Soviet Union where they'd stay hours to receive the murder signal. Fly along that line where he'd prepare his fingertips for the right combination as bombardier.

Under those whirling galaxies the mixture of LA and Asia and him being the wizard of the end of time cranked into his mother's starlet shape, he'd become this daylight pink rabbit, the only one who'd sighted the cross-hairs of the total death of being.

High Noon with that train whistle smashing down into your sternum or to switch channels for places like Phoenix where the Maiden, Aquanetta, who'd been saved in most of the Mexican D monster movies of the forties, was now advertising used Dodges for her car dealer husband in the same little girl voice she'd used to try to calm down Cihuacoatl, the starving one. Who existed on Earth as an obsidian knife, and sometimes the priests of her city would wrap her in a papoose bundle, send it to an innocent female vendor somewhere in the marketplace. She'd grow curious. Every time. They knew it. And knew she'd have to unwrap this infant, the knife that was the first thing born into the creation from the first mother to tell all the people that Heaven was thirsty again and waiting.

Every noon he'd be out on the street. The women and men amused by this rabbit among themselves. The sum and variety of their daily strain loosened for this time by sexual terms of the doll's appropriation of their lunch and all its pent up gestures. He became almost a grace to them, making it finally to the local gossip columns. Just walking. Waving. The adults flirting with the ambiguity. Pink furred. White tail. This rabbit who would have made them into poised shadows, the sinister glistening of another equation's outcome. And he knew it. Time eater among them and the rapture of disguise he carried. Almost time eater and the feast that was never his and the stories of the men no bigger than your eyelash growing into rotten giants that smother worlds.

Tom thought the Chalk Bluff's pictures looked like the dreams of a mind ruptured prince who coveted the desert so much that he went and turned into a jellyfish. The terror of those dreams and their energy seemed to be part of the daily life of the people who'd drawn them. Somehow they'd made themselves account for the communal nature of what rose out of their minds and made the cliff into that story no matter what the telling might bring them to. He'd thought if he sat on Mono Lake at the just right moment he'd trip into a story too, but all's he'd ever saw was a flash and the remnant energies floating into the distant reaches of the Earth's planetary edge. He'd light a cigarette, then row back to shore. If he felt like it, on the way back to his watering the rose fields, he'd stop and climb into a canyon and stack rocks in the shape of the B52s that he didn't have words for. Maybe an earthquake would make them twitch and fly maybe and maybe goddamned not. A is like its own sound when it aches. B is bags of cement when they've sat out too long in the rain. C is for cremation or any of those other words that have that letter stuck to their front end like them other Jews down the street and over the hill from the farmer with their tatoos and their knowledge of fire and the afterglow they have to live in, the aftertime they call home. At least they got to be the remains of themselves that they got to become. Tom and the farmer'd went to their group of houses once or twice with a pick-up full of sapling fruit trees.

✣

The singer at first liked what her voice could do. The way the song might float out of the body and rip a gash in the earth or scar a tree. She didn't know when these things would happen. Only that the song would come when she felt most voluptuous. If sometimes she could reach the multiple tones her throat produced out of one breath dividing itself, then the snakes would start arriving and she'd get scared because they wouldn't go away.

The lure of her voice at one end had no instructions at the other to reverse the calling she'd intoned in the multiple voicings her song had become. Everytime a song happened she would change slowly from herself at handsome knowingly hungry middle age to disease ravaged woman. Each song serving the transformation a little more, taking its time months or even years, that forward longing of her own breath, then back again to that point where she'd be the infant. Except to touch her in this state would mean instant and irreversible old age for the toucher. Her sons had been the first. When her song brought her back they were recognizable, but just that barrenness of its illumination made her tighten into the birth of herself, and then her sons, the heads and feet, and bodies that had come out of her. The gasping that she'd become then, and still the song wouldn't go away even when she begged it to, too terrified of that moment when it would treacherously arrive. The invisible substance of it forcing her mouth open, and lips to part it seemed for the song to hear itself that was trapped in her body.

She knew she was the first. No woman of her people had suffered this mouth play, and there were no words for it and what man would imagine himself with hands like these, invisible and angered, wanting so far only this hole in her body. She would go swimming in the canals outside the borders of her village. These were ditches, hundreds of years old, gouged out of the jungle by ancestral women who had the dreams of connecting these canals to the slow moving rivers that made their land come alive. Aquatic plants were grown there, and fish transferred from the wild to domestic water, and slowly birds came to eat the fish in the beginning, and then nest year round in the old trees that formed a canopy above the canals those first women had dug.

Slowly too, the frogs came, and worms and caimen and everything ate everything there, until the dredging time when all the festered death and waste had turned to precious mulch to be thrown on the fields and the dirt with it to be turned up and aired. Those women carrying loads, and stacking each handful into packed sour piles around the bases of the wild fruit trees they were studying, and how to attract the bees and flies and mosquitos to the new flowers. She'd swim in the oldest canals, but no caimen ever seemed hungry, no fish curious for the taste. The king one day, growing fearful over the stories of this woman, sent a professional drowner, his favorite who made a strange spectacle of ecstasy out of a breath looking for a body. He stayed in the jungle, never entering the village, watching only this woman, noting all her habits. But the song knew, and watched him, and he knew it slowly night after night until in terror he ran back to the king. The king was not angry at his drowner. He did not kill him, but instead had his hands tatooed and incised with the pictures of miracles. When that work had been done the king ordered the drowner's hands to be cut off and sent to the woman. The hands arrived in thickly wrapped palm leaves that were themselves wrapped in the most beautiful blanket the woman had ever seen. When the hands were unwrapped in front of her she began slowly to die. She told the women about the mouth play, about a future world that would be erected because of it and that even then it would not have a name.

FERRIT '93

THROUGH THE WIRE

TIM FERRET

+010+

In the dream, I'm waking. Tracking into a post-industrial holocaust—the world of man on fire. Here, emptiness is the essential commodity. Silence, except for the wind, our sole desire.

I'm waking to the songs of insects fucking in the decayed hair lining chipped toilet underbellies. Suitcases stuffed full of pit vipers—inside and out. All power lines are dead, but the wire still sings. Slack-jawed, we float in the night tethered to our half-severed, umbilical extension cords. Somewhere, through the white silence, music plays on…and it must stop.

I turn to the blood-splattered walls of the bathroom, its mottled Mickey Mouse wall paper is warped and peeled. A final mask can be seen even from here, bobbing softly in the overflowing tub. 'You've nothing to trust in.'

I have made key decisions about my death. I'll take it where and when I want. Nothing in this wretched dream can call the cards on me. I hold the hand that feeds and I bite it eagerly—savoring its sinewy flesh as I reach for another. I stare into the final mask, fondling wire, feeling its silent harmony. I scribble dead names along the walls and loose reptiles upon the sun-dead earth. In my dream, I'm awake in a dream. In the dream, we murder. Yes, we murder.

"Ready?" I grunt to Chase, securing the battered, dusty suitcase. He smiles, nods—he's half-mad and I love him like the brother I never wanted. Chase smears a hand across his face, then upward through his peroxide hair. Blood smears writhing runes across his forehead. Deciphered, I read only one word, 'Death.' Pursing my lips, I pick up my extension cords and begin wrapping them around my arms.

"How the fuck does anyone get lost in Kansas?" asks Chase, opening the screen door and stopping on the vacant porch. Outside the farmhouse, across the dusky road, I see our bicycles lying in the irrigation ditch where we abandoned them. "Especially us?"

-020-

As we pedal through the night, our respirators maxed out, I begin to hallucinate. We are hunting down the wires, they flex and rear like throngs of angry anacondas. Dreams are always nightmares in Kansas. I may not remember much, but I'll always remember that.

Below the bicycles movement is steady. The tires crunch softly through the migrating hordes of beetles. Chase hates every bit of it, but he has his reasons.

Moonlight reflects a shiny ribbon from chitinous shells. It twists into a river of scurrying movement which seems to go on forever.

Chase's breathing is heavy, his eyes are wild and cold. 'How far?' I hear him screaming silently. 'How far?' Chase wants to stop and lay prostrate in the shallow river of beetles. Chase bonds with what's left. He urinates to attract them, then defecates to feed them. He relishes the myriad spiked legs probing the hollows of his mouth. His sinus cavities are filled with insects. Sometimes they crawl out when he pretends to sleep. Can't relate to it. I only go in for reptiles, myself.

I recall every detail of the map inside my head, except the town's name. It's always been like this. I know this position, but I don't know how far. An uncertainty principle of psychic maps. I know distance only by the feel of the power lines, but they are all covered with beetles now. The power lines trail on and on along the roadside, the great inert network of the great dead plains. Yet, if I tighten the extension cords around my fists, I can feel the euphony through my hands. Perceiving static, I pedal on in hate toward the town.

+030+

Ripping the respirator from my face, I let the bicycle go out from beneath me and collapse in exhaustion under the heat of first light. There's another piece of dead tech here. A rusty water tower surrounded by barbed wire and dust. Nearby, a massive gridiron juts up into the bleak sky, overshadowing a viaduct, its broken facade stained orange and gray. I etch dead names across the abandoned concrete divide with my boot spurs. Chase grins and points to a rise of dust alongside my boot. "You're the reptile lover."

I spot the rattlesnake. As usual, the species is dislocated, found where it shouldn't be at all.

"Mexican?" asks Chase.

"Yeah," I breathe, slowly working one hand under the reptile while spinning an extension cord in the other. The animal buzzes and sways, its diamond eyes hatefully locked with my own. 'Funny,' I think, 'you threaten me, yet caress my hand.' I lift the snake and walk to one of the suitcases mounted on the back of my bicycle.

"I don't care what anyone says," Chase yells, "you're still the best I've ever seen!" From across the plains the dusters blow, carrying the scent of a single rider. Chase smiles and moves out of sight with his bicycle.

"Horseman," I hiss, watching as the rattler churns slow circles across my outstretched hands. The lone rider heads in our direction. As the rider nears, my vision clears into the dream and I'm no longer that which I am. I become only that which I must deliver. The appaloosa snorts and bucks as it draws to a halt. The rider's duster jacket flaps loudly in the wind. He does not bother to remove his respirator. He only raises a rifle and takes aim from behind the dark lens of his mask.

"I love you," I say, curling a lip as he steadies the weapon's barrel. Holding the rattler out to the horseman, I slowly begin to move in his direction.

"Stand and die where you are! You murderer! You sick fuck!" He pulls the trigger as Chase appears behind the horse and wrenches him off his saddle. My hallucinations begin when the bullet passes through my skull. I dream that the mass of my head is exploded across the plain behind me, but I do not feel pain. Grinning, I approach his cowering form and he twirls, rolling away from the horse. But Chase is already there. He smiles and spiders crawl out from behind his rotting teeth. They scurry down his neck and disappear behind his collar as he steps on the rider's stomach.

I kneel and, with my free hand, strip away the horseman's mask. He gazes up into my eyes, the scent of his fright exciting the rattler. There's much to be loved in the final mask. Much to be cherished in my reflection trapped in the glassy rounds of his eyes. "You're only a man, but I love you," I whisper, as the snake strikes one and he screams. "Tick-tock-tick-tock-tick-tock."

As the man wildly thrashes about, Chase guts the horse with his spurs and my hallucinations weaken. The appaloosa folds to the ground, its cries becoming more feeble with every shallow breath. The rider's neck swells purple from venom racing to his heart. The fang punctures in his face gape like multiple sets of bloodied, defiant eyes. I somberly watch as the snake oozes away on the sun-baked terrain.

Chase stops disemboweling the horse and stares open-mouthed at the power lines along the road's shoulder. I, too, connect with the silent roar. The heat hurts my ears, but not as much as the music which plays on and on.

-040-

Dreaming in twilight, my guts are swollen—heavy with raw horse and rider. From where I float all directions are horizons, as if I am centered in an endless bowl. On the plain before me stands the cross we erected, adorned with razor wire, hearts and lengths of intestine. This is Chase's creation, his dream—his beautiful and elegant monument.

I stretch, flexing the wire wrapped around my arms. Making a garrote, I snap it between my hands. "How I long to use my extension cords," I quietly tell the night. A rustle from behind causes me to ground my feet. I know it's Chase. 'There's nothing to trust,' I tell myself, turning to look into his eyes.

"How far?" Chase asks.

"Dawn," I answer, spinning a cord as I approach my bicycle. The insects are restless, already they cover the power lines and most of the road's surface. Furrowing a brow, I look

down and begin picking at the paint chips along the bicycle's frame. "Put them away. I'm not in the mood."

He giggles, fitting the respirator over his face. His laugh is rich, melodic, and terrifying. Shaking my head, I, too, begin to laugh. Waving goodbye to our cross, we pedal into the darkness.

Time has emptied out of the dream and us. The texture of the road is at the timeless center of my dream. The hallucinations are more vivid now. I feel the power of what I am. Chase whistles softly and rolls his eyes at me. I watch in a rear-view mirror as he drops behind, folding into the fabric of the night.

I lean forward over the handlebars and arch my back until I'm staring straight up at the sky. The shape I'm looking for is preceded by its sound, the creaking whir of a rusty chain. I scan the machine with my eyes, identifying it as a da Vinci glider. The running lights are weak, but I've little doubt I've been spotted. I quickly stop the bicycle and unravel an extension cord. The da Vinci comes in low enough for me to hurl the twenty-five foot line. The cord snags the operator's foot and wraps around a pedal. I'm dragged along the road, like a small child with an unruly kite, but my pull slows the glider to a stall. I hear the swift approach of Chase's laughter as he races to the vehicle's point of impact. Insects cloud his wake as he passes on his bicycle. Releasing my hold on the cord, the da Vinci surges forward and plummets to the road.

+050+

In the dream I'm awake. Awake, I stalk the earth, but it's ten thousand years ago. Sometimes, in the waking, I'm no longer living flesh. My flesh always lives in the dream, crawling in tiny fleshy circles, encapsulating heart and soul.

The immanence of our blessed acts, our gifts of fortune—these splendors of the damned—gives us joy to celebrate. We regard all life, however delicate, however wondrous, original or unique, as so much cherishable dust.

I dream in the time of plague, a dark age where all machines have failed. Waste blackens the skies and suffocates the oceans. Queen Flora's dead now. Only the vipers and the insect kings rule. I dream of a Holy War where death crusades and I am its deliverance. In this, the year of our Lord, 2040, all life is passing—flooding out into the darkness of our being. Only the fallen angels can tell you, only the fallen angels know.

"Tick-tock-tick-tock-tick," I whisper. Torn souls like an ancient tapestry flicker brightly and charge the air around me. In their golden light, one hand on my heart and the other outstretched—wrapped in extension cords—I gaze upon the collapsed da Vinci. Chase stands behind me, his hands slowly working my crotch as he watches the aviator crawl from the wreck. The aviator's legs are broken and he's in great pain. Not for long in the dream, but for an eternity of waking.

"How far?" asks Chase.

"The span of the road," I murmur as he licks my neck, "but we've nothing to trust." I pull away in sudden disinterest and bob my head, moving toward the aviator.

"Killing me won't do any good!" he cries. "They know about you! Everybody does! They're waiting. Oh God, please don't kill me—please! I—I can help! I know how to—"

His urine attracts the armored insect conquistadors. Their watchful silhouettes contour the dream's horizons. His fright provokes me. Snakes slither forth from the wounds in my hands and feet to greet him.

"No—don't, please, I—," Picking him up by his head, I lean in, locking our mouths together. His eyes are wide as my tongue explores his tiny mouth. His mouth is tight, like my anus. Chase senses my desire. He violently grabs me from behind, plunging his sex into my rectum. His fucking is savage, full of abandon. He growls, convulsively thrusting his hips and letting saliva roll down my back. Suddenly an explosion of cold, spikey insects fires through my bowels, but tonight I do not mind.

Tears fall from the aviator's eyes. He makes muffled grunting sounds as I let my tongue unfurl in his mouth. It's a snake now, a viper, much like Chase's penis. The viper expands and the aviator's jaws snap like brittle twigs between my hands.

Chase disengages as I let the aviator fall to the ground. He's not purified yet—he still slithers at my feet and soils the earth. He makes gurgling sounds as he tries to crawl away.

"You understand our love for you." I smile at the aviator. "You've nothing else to trust in anymore."

"A fairy tale ending," Chase says. Buckets of cockroaches explode from his mouth as he speaks. The hungry insects hit the ground and race toward the aviator. "Written in hell."

I bend over, thrusting my hand into the blanket of insects covering the aviator's chest. Chase plunges his mantis-cock into me as I punch through the aviator's rib cage. I feel his warm heart and pluck it like an apple from a small tree. Chase discharges his dream inside me as I roll my eyes and bite down on the pulsing, scarlet organ. Chase peers over my shoulder and I place the remainder of the aviator's heart on his tongue. Together, we smile, then abruptly disengage.

We impart our vision of beauty upon the da Vinci. Then the dream begins to fade. For a fleeting instant, we seem like nothing more than two lost and lonely souls standing along an abandoned roadside. For a moment, I hate Chase even more than I hate myself.

We finish the da Vinci. It's a cross now, garnished with the aviator's intestines and brain. I take the aviator's skull and examine it. Tearing open my own head, I place the aviator's inside. I try to see through his skull, but cannot. I can only trace his vision. The aviator's skull feels sad and alone, as forsaken as the world.

-060-

"Dawn," I announce, loosening the suitcase straps at the rear of my bicycle.

"It's how far we've come," answers Chase. He levitates, legs folded against his chest, arms wrapped around them. Several feet below him is a boulder. It's the only boundary between the town and our hate.

"Population 824," I say, turning in a crouch and snapping a garrote-extension cord between my hands, "but dropping fast."

"You incurable plaguester!" Chase laughs. "About time you lightened up."

"I always lighten up now." In the dream, the music is very near and I can almost understand its voice.

"People await us," says Chase, intently staring at the horizon, "with open arms."

Opening a suitcase, I balefully survey its contents. I dream of iron gags, oral pears, skinning cats and Spanish spiders. Of hanging cages, cat's paws, tongs and knee-splitters, too. Inside the decaying, ancient box rests sharp, toothy saws, breaking wheels and extension cords—everything I require. Lifting a rusty head-crusher, I closely examine its spikes before fastening it on my shoulder. I carefully inspect every tool. I must, the dream is very strong.

Chase watches as I remove the second suitcase from my bicycle. This one I will open only when the time is right. "Music?" he asks, furrowing a brow.

I look across the barren plain, through the dusters languidly winding away across the exhausted soil, into the distant dream. Twirling cords around my body, I recognize the call more clearly than before. "It's there," I answer bitterly, picking up my suitcase. "We'll walk."

We move across the terrain, our smiles growing wider as our visions stream out of us. The pores of the dying earth gasp, exhaling swarms of insects into the thin air. Chase herds them before us, assuming the aspect of a diseased black fly. His compound eyes and smiling mandibles are crawling with myriad tiny black flies as he thrusts his scarecrow arms before him. A roaring buzz deafens my ears. It's a death song full of beauty and terror, orchestrated to provoke the dream.

I see the faces of the gathered. They are lined up with guns and scythes, armored with their illusions of strength, power and destiny. But our aspects cause them to sense the utter hopelessness of the dream. I hold the suitcase before me, knowing the time is now right. The suitcase trembles and smokes. A town woman's scream hangs in the air as the suitcase blasts open, firing a river of half-rotted, half-alive reptiles toward the town. The suitcase signals our angelic strategy—the townspeople break rank and run, an occasional volley of gunfire marking retaliation in their retreat.

We slowly move forward, ten feet above the ground, as bullets tear through our dream-flesh and bone. From each hole gouging my body a snake struggles forward, its venomous mouth gaping and wide beneath an eyeless skull. The insects reach the town before we do. Everyone scampers in the pandemonium before the slaughter. Some townspeople raise barrels to their heads. They pull the trigger—they cannot wait for the dream to end. Still others try to fight, because they cannot surrender their dream.

"Only the fallen angels can tell you, only the fallen angels know," I sing from above, my arms outstretched in the golden light—toward their dead names. "You've nothing to trust in anymore."

The endless screaming begins. Chase takes my hand in his. As one, we smile and descend.

+070+

In the post-industrial holocaust, all the world's afire. We murder. But now we hear only the hollow cries of the wind.

"We're in a state of entropic disarray. Our wings are unkempt and rotting—irreversible decay." Chase's black eyes flash as he turns slow circles in the air before me. His wings are lifeless appendages, black and crisp, yet also fetid and damp. They are as beautiful to me as my own—and we slowly spin....

From below, blood and dust churns up to embrace our feet. Everywhere, bodies slowly slip down pikes or hang from hand-fashioned crosses. Beneath barbed wire crowns, mouths are spread as wide as abdomens and the infinite Kansas sky. Every heart has been nailed to the rooftops or hung on front porch doors. Some still pulse in the sunset of our dream.

Witness this triumph, this defeat of the dream. Our labors have been long and hard, deserving of every reward. Now we are nearing dream's end. We have great cause to celebrate, as only the fallen angels know. We spin. We spin and we spin. All final masks have been exposed. Suddenly we stop.

"Tick-tock-tick-tock-tick-tock," I whisper, watching Saint Elmo's fire gambol about my fingertips and extension cords. "Except the very *final* mask."

"How far?" Chase's black eyes swirl red, then black again.

"Ensue the road," I answer, looking toward the abandoned town square. At the square's center stands a four-spired church. The entrance under the cinquefoil arch is open, spilling shadows across the portal. In the crimson light of dusk, all is silent save for the music flowing from the temple hall. Blue sparks surge before me and my cords begin to sing. Still the voice lilts on, a symphony tracing veins of wire which bind, cohere and communicate with our toppled souls. I'm intoxicated, reeling in the ecstasy of the call. Chase feels it, too. We hold no hatred for the dream now, only a desire to understand the music.

-080-

We enter the church, pausing in the narthex to view the empty aisles. I'm now spinning a dozen extension cords, watching the electric blue lighting race across the hall's interior.

Chase flutters forward, suddenly stopping to look back at the entrance doors. "We shouldn't—"

"Go," I move by him to the crossing. The hall is glorious to behold. Inset lozenge windows radiate like novas trapped in amber lancets. Lush red carpet spills like blood from the chancel rail, down the stairs, and main aisle. The pews shimmer, as if their wooden legs and feet are rooted through the floor and into the earth below. Chase joins me. We hover at the altar, before the Cross of Christ. Our wounds mimic his stigmata, pouring out blood and insects, as we arch our backs to the ceiling.

Chase's wings brush the tabernacle and it opens. Saint Elmo's fire walks around the pix as Chase reaches for the chalice. The voice grows louder as we hold our hands above the chalice, letting our blood fill the cup. Chase laughs and peels a slice of flesh from his chest. I follow, placing the bread of my body on the paten.

After blessing our flesh, Chase takes a firm hold on me and forces his sex into the wound in my side. My whirling extension cords are moving so fast they can no longer be seen. They spin through our joined bodies, but we do not notice them. We slowly fuck, turning end on end in the air as we place each other's offering in our mouths. The Communion flesh turns to stone on our tongues, but we swallow it because it is ours.

Chase quickens his thrusts into my wound while violently gripping my genitals. Lifting the chalice to my mouth, I notice a small box over Chase's shoulder. The box is resting at the base of the crucifix. Chase stops, turning to gaze at the device.

Moving closer, I realize the box is a small radio. The voice emanates from its tiny speaker in pure static. As we concentrate on the white noise, the extension cords sing its message, translating the sonic spectrum into words. Chase's eyes lock with mine as he tries to pull away, but we are caught—entangled in the extension cords—forced to understand the static message.

"No," I cry, as the singing corners me in the dream, shredding my putrid wings, stripping me of true vision. Chase screams, horrified by his climax of nothing more than hot, milky liquid across my thigh. Through the deafening roar, we struggle, we beg for mercy. We plead on our hands and knees before the silent radio, but we are all alone.

+090+

In the smoking ruins of the church, we squat before the charred Cross of Christ. The cross stands alone, silhouetted by the last rays of light forsaken by the setting sun. In the shadows, we babble to ourselves and crawl naked through the hot ash.

I lift the shattered plastic radio, examining its severed cord. Chase's eyes gleam like a pair of full moons, as he pulls himself up with a thick piece of wood. A long spike protrudes from one end of the board. He uses it as a handle to lean upon. Mortal blood trickles from the cuts on our bodies. My vagina and breasts mark me as nothing more than a woman—a mere woman. I look at Chase with tears in my eyes. "Deserted! That's what we are! Stripped and abandoned!" I pound my trembling fists on the shards of radio, letting the plastic cut into my fingers and wrist. "Rape!" I hysterically scream. "Rape and murder!"

Chase steps forward, his eyes rolled back in his skull as he raises the spiked board above his head. "If I had a ticket to heaven," he chants, "and you didn't have one, too. I'd throw my ticket to heaven away, and go to hell with you!"

Swinging the board down from his shoulder, Chase impales me with the spike. I stagger backward, the iron peg's deathly iciness immediately pervades my gut. As I fall against the cross, the statue is scraped by the metal tip protruding from my back.

Chase advances, his hands wildly clawing the air before him as he gropes for my throat. "No!" I gasp, pulling myself behind the cross. I lean against the statue of Christ until I feel it slip. The Cross of Christ rolls forward off its base and the crown of Jesus' head rams into Chase's, shattering his skull and knocking him to the ground. I shiver, watching as his blood pools out at my feet and his last breath escapes him.

Clutching the spiked board to my abdomen, I stumble away, leaving the ruins of the church and town behind.

-000-

I totter toward the thin red line of light carving out the horizon. Repulsion causes it to retract at my touch. My mouth is dry, eyes are wet. Slowly, I realize the creaking sound I hear isn't distant music, but the rattling of my lungs. I'm dying, but I laugh hysterically while thrusting my exhausted frame across the pointless span before me.

I collapse face down in the dust, caressing the cross of spike and wood attached to me. The cross hurts as much as I, so I comfort it until the end. I assure myself, lying at the edge of the dream, "You've nothing to trust in anymore."

LADY-BOY

JILL ST. JACQUES

I have friends in Bangkok.

I can see one lone white chicken in the yard. Daybreak starts with that, and cold rainwater in a pot. The stomache isn't awake yet, can't hold down food, not yet. I always knew she was into heroine—it was her humor, her eyes. I think of Bangkok, of those plastic floral print tablecloths with red roses like smashed mouths, my transsexual prostitute lover nodding on heroin in the corner where they stack green Sprite bottles in red cases, level of green, level of red, up to the ceiling, high.

I order a Sprite. I nod. The waiter pours it into a plastic baggie, slips a clear straw inside, and with a deft rhythmic flick snaps a fleshy rubber band around its neck. The completed assemblage is a weird sparkling I.V. unit. I plunge the straw between the slit of my sticky hummingbird hummingjob lips, and I suck on that bag, I probe and suck on that mosquito sparklebag of Sprite until it's just a corner of the bag. It tastes cold, tastes plastic, tastes good.

The waiter returns the Sprite bottle to one of the red cases in the green and red tower.

Deposit money. Bottles. Green glass.

The prostitute nods up. Her eyes are bleak periods, sensuous, final. She has little beads of sweat on her upper lip. It's not a hot day. It's heroine sweat. Not too hot. "Mai phet." When the wolf came, Little Thai Red Riding Hood opened up the door. It's not really hot. When it's really hot in Bangkok, the flies skate slowly across the peanut sauce, lazy, torpid, the tropic of heroine. Little Thai Red Riding hood said come on in big bad wolf. I want to fuck your teeth. I want to fuck those teeth you have. Big white hearse teeth.

The sweat on our lips is elegant.
wee wee wee is almost all the way home

Big bad wolf, come right on in. She nods. You've given up. Katoi. Katoi is what the Khon-Thai call us: lady-boy. Katoi mean red rose red halter top red ice cream stick red cinnamon candy red lipstick smile red asshole red pussyhole where Little Red Riding Hood looked big bad wolf in the eye. "This is for the fifth little piggie," she said and eased down soft on Bad Wolf's fang. "I'll fuck all your pretty teeth one by one," her elegant sweat limps down her leg, her thigh scarred beautiful peaceful furrows, a farm for other teeth, other money, other time.

Little Red Sleeping Beauty lets Wolf seize her wicked witch tits, her wicked witch cock. The Wolf can't get a hard on, so he watches, beats off in feeble strokes. When wicked witch katoi boy gets it in her little red asshole her little wicked witch dick gets hard hard hard. Wicked witch black haired dick so hard you flick it it goes dick goes hard...twock! Like cantaloupe. Pock! Hard dick swells so very hot, so very wicked witch hard.

Oedipus had no eyes.

The dick was severed, end to end. Hollowed out dug out like a canoe. But in the old days they burned them out, it was the only way. Camels hump. The dick suffers, severed, hollowed out. Now the dick is severed. You take out the muscle. The meat is taken out. Folds are made. The little lamb is taken into the fold. Folded in naked. The little lamb squirms. Little Red Sleeping Beauty anaesthetized, scalpeled, neat and nice. Now we make a hole. The hole is a lie, it's more of a sleeve. Seeds. No more seeds. There is a hole, the hole is a lie, there is a sleeve, there is no seed in the sleeve. It is folded, tucked, nice and neat, and now bed-time beckons us all. Goodnight Tink. Good-night Tinkerbell. G'night Peter.

The most sensitive part of the penis is the rough orange peel underside of the head, soft underbelly of the snake, encrusted with jewels, like a dragon, like a soft sleeping dragon the penis is opened up. The soft underside underhead scalpel neatly divides. Clitoris. Construct clitoris: (scar). Construct vulva-sleeves: (scar). Rose is the tablecloth, rose is the scar, rose in the cherry, rose in the hole, the throne is divided, the table is set, and now we invite you to dinner.

Now the fat German auto-parts salesman comes to the feast. He brings us his money. You didn't like cock, but you will like this, because you are an idiot and you don't know who you're fucking. I'm not talking about me, I'm far too big. I have a big fat cock, and I will kill you with it. I am katoi. I am Ladyboy, but I am Big Sister Ladyboy, you understand?

I have friends in Bangkok, friends are little sister. You will like little sister ladyboy, I know you will. Little lady has slit you like. You pretend man. You never know. Me you know.

Big shoulders you know. Bad wolf. Bad bad wolf. Little sister tucked neat. Tucked clean. Slide in mouths of white linen. Touch little sister. You like?

The table is set, the fool has come to feast. You fool. You never know how we laugh at you, big cock man. We laugh and laugh and laugh. You are not katoi. You have no little sister. You have no eyes.

We are cats. We lick ourselves clean.

Pardon me, big cock auto parts man, but I think you are bewitched. You have been talking to alligators again. What do you talk about with those alligators? Auto parts? Suitcases? Luggage? Wallets? Shoes? Things that you slide your stuff into. Alligator pumps. Alligator shirts. It's hot out now. Now it's really hot. The mosquitoes fan softly cool bloated thorax—if the blood is too hot, the mosquito will melt. All that's left is the eyes.

Poor Oedipus.

Oedipus has no eyes.

He's all gutted now, that's final.

The katoi prostitute head fall so close to plate of shrimp glass noodle, sof' ping sheem. Glass Thai ice coffee no touch now. A fine misty sweat on the dark down of her arms. Good heroine for katoi. Katoi pen dii. Katoi pen dii pro-wa katoi dag fin. Katoi dag fin mak-mak, katoi dag fin mak le fin pen dii kaa. Katoy suay, le katoi dag fin. Katoi suay.

Oedipus. Where did your vision go?

They call our business "skinning the gecko."

Where did that vision go?

The gecko is a soft beige lizard with large cute eyes like droplets of silicone and a pink flickery tongue. It is said if you grab a gecko by the tail and snap it snap it down, the soft beige skin will tear off in one long piece. Like a glove. Like a bad boy's pajamas. That skin come off fine, like a gecko, like a glove.

Skinning the gecko by the swimming pool. I am big sister katoi. Your dollah mean nuthin to me. All the better to eat you with, dearie. What big tits you have, Granny. All the better to skin you with, dearie. My what thick oozy make-up you have Granny. My what stout arms. My what cleft chin. My what big feet.

I am big ugly sister katoi, gecko man, I look out for me and little sister.

If the blood is too hot, the mosquito will melt.

INTRODUCING THE BLACK ICE BOOKS SERIES:

The Black Ice Books Series will introduce readers to the new generation of dissident writers in revolt. Breaking out of the age-old traditions of mainstream literature, the voices published here are at once ribald, caustic, controversial, and inspirational. These books signal a reflowering of the art underground. They explore iconoclastic styles that celebrate life vis-à-vis the spirit of their unrelenting energy and anger. Similar to the recent explosion in the alternative music scene, these books point toward a new counterculture rage that's just now finding its way into the mainstream discourse. The Black Ice Books Series brings to readers the most radical fiction being written in America today.

The Kafka Chronicles

A novel by Mark Amerika

The Kafka Chronicles investigates the world of passionate sexual experience while simultaneously ridiculing everything that is false and primitive in our contemporary political discourse. Mark Amerika's first novel ignites hyper-language that explores the relationship between style and substance, self and sexuality, and identity and difference. His energetic prose uses all available tracks, mixes vocabularies, and samples genres. Taking its cue from the recent explosion of angst-driven rage found in the alternative rock music scene, this book reveals the unsettled voice of America's next generation.

Mark Amerika has lived in Florida, New York, California, and different parts of Europe, and has worked as a free-lance bicycle courier, lifeguard, video cameraman, and grey-hound racing official. Amerika's fiction has appeared in many magazines, including *Fiction International*, *Witness*, the German publication *Lettre International*, and *Black Ice*, of which he is editor. He is presently writing a "violent concerto for deconstructive guitar" in Boulder, Colorado.

"Mark Amerika not only plays music—the rhythm, the sound of his words and sentences—he plays verbal meanings as if they're music. I'm not just talking about music. Amerika is showing us that William Burroughs came out of jazz knowledge and that now everything's political—and everything's coming out through the lens of sexuality..."

—*Kathy Acker*

Paper, ISBN: 0-932511-54-6, $7.00

Revelation Countdown

Short Fiction by Cris Mazza

While in many ways reaffirming the mythic dimension of being on the road already romaticized in American pop and folk culture, *Revelation Countdown* also subtly undermines that view. These stories project onto the open road not the nirvana of personal freedom but rather a type of freedom more closely resembling loss of control. Being in constant motion and passing through new environments destabilizes life, casts it out of phase, heightens perception, skews reactions. Every little problem is magnified to overwhelming dimensions; events segue from slow motion to fast forward; background noises intrude, causing perpetual wee-hour insomnia. In such an atmosphere, the title *Revelation Countdown,* borrowed from a roadside sign in Tennessee, proves prophetic: It may not arrive at 7:30, but revelation will inevitably find the traveler.

Cris Mazza is the author of two previous collections of short fiction, *Animal Acts* and *Is It Sexual Harassment Yet?* and a novel, *How to Leave a Country*. She has resided in Brooklyn, New York; Clarksville, Tennessee; and Meadville, Pennsylvania; but she has always lived in San Diego, California.

"...fictions that are remarkable for the force and freedom of their imaginative style."

—New York Times Book Review

Paper, ISBN: 0-932511-73-2, $7.00

Avant-Pop: Fiction for a Daydream Nation
Edited by Larry McCaffery

In *Avant-Pop,* Larry McCaffery has assembled a collection of innovative fiction, comic book art, illustrations, and various unclassifiable texts written by the most radical and subversive literary talents of the postmodern new wave. The authors included here vary in background, from those with well-established reputations as cult figures in the pop underground (Samuel R. Delany, Kathy Acker, Ferret, Derek Pell, Harold Jaffe), to important new figures who have gained prominence since the late eighties (Mark Leyner, Eurudice, William T. Vollmann), to, finally, the most promising new kids on the block.

Avant-Pop is meant to send a collective wake-up call to all those readers who spent the last decade nodding off, along with the rest of America's daydream nation. To those readers and critics who have decried the absence of genuinely radicalized art capable of liberating people from the bland roles and assumptions they've accepted in our B-movie society of the spectacle, *Avant-Pop* announces that reports about the death of the literary avant-garde have been greatly exaggerated.

Larry McCaffery, "Guru of the Interview" (*American Book Review*) and "Guru of the Po-Mo Overview" (*Mondo 2000*), recently published *Storming the Reality Studio: A Casebook of Cyberpunk and Postmodern SF* and *Across the Wounded Galaxies: Interviews with Contemporary American SF Writers.*

Paper, ISBN: 0-932511-72-4, $7.00

New Noir

Stories by John Shirley

In *New Noir,* John Shirley, like a postmodern Edgar Allen Poe, depicts minds deformed into fantastic configurations by the pressure, the very weight, of an entire society bearing down on them. "Jody and Annie on TV," selected by the editor of *Mystery Scene* as "perhaps the most important story...in years in the crime fiction genre," reflects the fact that whole segments of zeitgeist and personal psychology have been supplanted by the mass media, that the average kid on the streets in Los Angeles is in a radical crisis of exploded self-image, and that life really is meaningless for millions. The stories here also bring to mind Elmore Leonard and the better crime novelists, but John Shirley—unlike writers who attempt to extrapolate from peripheral observation and research—bases his stories on his personal experience of extreme people and extreme mental states, and his struggle with the seductions of drugs, crime, prostitution, and violence.

John Shirley was born in Houston, Texas in 1953 but spent the majority of his youth in Oregon. He has been a lead singer in a rock band, Obsession, writes lyrics for various bands, including Blue Oyster Cult, and in his spare time records with the Panther Moderns. He is the author of numerous works in a variety of genres; his story collection *Heatseeker* was chosen by the Locus Reader's Poll as one of the best collections of 1989. His latest novel is *Wetbones.*

"John Shirley serves up the bloody heart of a rotting society with the aplomb of an Aztec surgeon on Dexedrine."

—*ALA Booklist*

Paper, ISBN: 0-932511-55-4, $7.00